ON THE MARRAM SHORE

Catriona Dunbar is sent to stay with relatives on the Lancashire coast for the season. But between perpetually drunken Samuel Espley and his caddish son Julian, life in the grand house of Pelham is far from the happy holiday she had been anticipating. The only consolation is her growing friendship with the hired hand Morgan Chappel: a bond that seems poised to blossom into something more. Until Morgan is arrested — and Catriona must make a devil's bargain to save him . . .

JUNE DAVIES

◆

ON THE
MARRAM
SHORE

Complete and Unabridged

LINFORD
Leicester

First published in Great Britain in 1994

First Linford Edition
published 2019

A catalogue record for this book is available
from the British Library.

ISBN 978–1–4448–4191–6

Published by
F. A. Thorpe (Publishing)
Anstey, Leicestershire

Set by Words & Graphics Ltd.
Anstey, Leicestershire
Printed and bound in Great Britain by
T. J. International Ltd., Padstow, Cornwall

This book is printed on acid-free paper

1

Catriona Dunbar stood before her window at Pelham, tying the frayed ribbons of her camisole as she stared down across the wet gardens and beyond the weathered gate to the shore fields with their tall, coarse grasses and clumps of hardy sea hollies.

The tide was ebbing, the power of its great crashing waves spent as it receded, flat and grey and pin-cushioned with fine needles of November rain. A brigantine with furled sails bound for Liverpool was blurry on the distant horizon, almost like a ghost ship.

Catriona had been a little girl when she was plucked from the churning sea and dragged aboard a rowboat by rescuers who had put out from Friars Quay, but the lives of her parents had been amongst the many lost that stormy spring night.

It all seemed so very long ago, and yet . . .

From the corner of her eye, Catriona glimpsed the paleness of her wedding gown, laid across the high, narrow bed. She shivered. The past often haunted her now.

Catriona's hazel eyes darkened with despair — whom had she to blame but herself?

The bedroom door swung open and a young maidservant, wearing a faded dress covered by a voluminous, patched apron, entered briskly.

'Mister Julian's nearly finished breakfast, and he said, why haven't you come down?'

'Not this morning, Eliza.'

The maid nodded, taking Catriona's stays and petticoats from the dresser drawer. ''Thought not, ma'am. It's bad luck to see the bridegroom on the day of the wedding — I told Mister Julian that, but he wouldn't listen. Just roared with laughter and said I was

2

spouting nonsense.'

Catriona stepped into the petticoats Eliza held, standing quite still while the maid fastened the ties.

It was indeed a wry quirk of fate which had thrown the two women together this way. After the suspicions and jealousies that had once existed between them, Eliza was the nearest to a friend Catriona had left in the world.

A quick knot of tension tightened within Catriona. By the day's end, this room would no longer be hers. After the marriage ceremony that evening, she'd be expected to share the master bedroom with Julian Espley.

'There, ma'am!' Eliza said, smoothing down the layers of petticoats with her work-roughened hands. 'Got the tiniest waist in the whole county, I reckon.'

Catriona heard the catch in the maid's voice, and looked around quickly. Eliza at once turned away, but not before Catriona had glimpsed the pensive expression in her eyes.

'Eliza . . . ' she began awkwardly.

'*Don't*, ma'am!' The maid's face was drawn and sallow in the dull light cast by the candles. 'Don't pity me, I can't bear it. 'Sides, it's not the wedding — well, not only that, anyhow.'

'Then what?' persisted Catriona gently, impulsively closing her own small hands about Eliza's larger, rougher ones.

Eliza chewed the inside of her cheek anxiously. 'He's back, ma'am!' she blurted at last. 'I wasn't sure whether to say nothing — but he's back!'

'Morgan . . . ' The name fell as a whisper from Catriona's lips as she stared in disbelief at Eliza. She felt colour draining from her face. Her legs were suddenly too weak to support her weight, and she gripped the carved bedpost, sinking down heavily onto the corner of the mattress.

'Where is he?'

'I saw him down on the shore, ma'am.'

'If Morgan's caught here in Friars

4

Quay, he'll hang, Eliza!' Catriona almost choked on the words. 'After such a long time having passed, I thought — prayed — he would surely have left the country.' She turned questioning eyes upon Eliza. 'Whatever can have brought him back to Pelham?'

'Only one reason there can be, I reckon,' commented Eliza. 'Your wedding.'

'Did you talk to him?' Catriona's heart was pounding.

The maid gave her an incredulous look. 'I surely did not! Morgan didn't even see me, miss. I made certain of *that*!'

Catriona could well understand that Eliza might be shocked — dismayed, even — by Morgan's return. However, she was mystified by the peculiar emotion she read in the other girl's face.

'Eliza, you're afraid!' she murmured. 'But why? Morgan would never hurt you! What reason would he have to bear you a grievance? If anyone has cause to fear him,' she went on in a low voice, 'it is I. After all, it was my word sent him to gaol. That Morgan is now an escaped convict who must always hide and be hunted is *my* doing.'

'Aye, but we don't — ' Eliza broke off in alarm, and Catriona's senses lurched at the heavy footsteps bearing down along the landing.

'Eliza! Where the devil *are* you, girl?'

'It's only Julian!' Catriona's sigh of relief was clearly audible.

In the next instant, Julian Espley's fist was pounding on Catriona's door.

'I thought I'd find you in here gossiping!' Julian's impatience was directed at Eliza. 'I'm already late. Where are my boots?'

Eliza glowered at him. 'I put them out for you, sir. After I'd cleaned them.'

'Well, I can't find them! Don't just stand there gawping, go and fetch 'em for me!'

The maid stamped from the room to do as she was bidden.

'I've urgent business in Liverpool,

Catriona, but I shall be home in good time for the ceremony.' With a wicked grin, Julian left Catriona to her troubled thoughts.

When she was alone once more, Catriona returned to the lattice-paned window. Her knuckles whitened as she gripped the ledge, not wishing to recall the very last occasion on which she had seen Morgan Chappel — crouching dirty, ragged, and utterly humiliated in the vile filth of a crowded prison cell.

Other memories swam before her. Sharply vivid pictures of the day, almost three years ago, when Catriona had discovered she was to visit Pelham . . .

2

Brilliant sunshine reflecting from fresh-fallen snow was filtering through the stained glass, its golden light suffusing the mossy, rough-stone kirk in the Highland village of Strathlachie, and glowing upon the serious faces of the small choir.

Oliver Stuart abruptly raised his bony hands from the keys of the organ, and snapped his shrewd eyes upon the two rows of singers.

'No, no, *no!*' he said tersely.

Mr Stuart's stern gaze raked the back row of male voices, lingering purposefully upon the earnest, rather pale features of Robert Mathieson. Sensing the scrutiny, Robert shuffled uncomfortably, lowering his eyes as he felt his smooth cheeks burning.

'Let's try again, choir,' Mr Stuart instructed, adding sharply: 'And softly, this time. Softly!'

The instant the choirmaster's attention was focused upon his playing, Robert Mathieson cautiously leaned forward to the row of women and girl singers, and gently tugged one of Catriona Dunbar's glossy, flaxen braids.

Fifteen-year-old Catriona started, raising her hazel eyes from her music book, but not daring to look around. She felt a slight tug upon her braid once again, and then a small, folded square of thick paper was tossed over her right shoulder, landing with a clumsy bounce onto the open pages of her book.

Catriona stifled a gasp of surprise, her eyes now fixed upon the choirmaster's back as she endeavoured to slide the paper from her book and into the safety of her palm without it rustling or being seen by keen-eyed Mr Stuart.

Sophy Hamilton elbowed Catriona in the ribs, mouthing, *Well done!* when Catriona chanced to glance sidelong at her best friend.

'It was just so funny! I thought I was going to *burst*!' Sophy exploded once practice was over and the girls were fetching their coats. 'When Robbie's note bounced that way — oh, my! I thought it was surely going to tumble right down and hit Mr Stuart on his bald pate!' She lowered her voice confidentially. 'What does it say?'

'I haven't read it yet,' answered Catriona, as they started out from the kirk. 'I'll open it — '

'Miss Dunbar!'

Catriona turned around, pausing on the kirk's worn stone steps as the choirmaster hurried after her, wrapping a muffler about his long neck.

'Miss Dunbar, I wanted to ask after your grandmother. Is she feeling better?'

'Very much, thank you, Mr Stuart.' Catriona smiled. Essie McPherson had been extremely poorly, but was at last on the mend. 'Doctor Milne sees Granny every day, but he's pleased with her recovery.'

10

'You might tell Essie I'll be sure to come by for a visit.' The choirmaster raised his hat and started away through the deep, frosty snow towards the manse. 'Cheer her up a wee bit.'

Sophy grimaced, leaning close to Catriona's ear. 'If I was ill, a visit from vinegary old Oliver Stuart would see me off altogether!'

'He's only being kind, Sophy,' reproved Catriona mildly.

The girls had become firm friends since Catriona first arrived in Strathlachie as a wee girl to live with her Grand- mother McPherson. Despite the girls' characters being as different as chalk from cheese, Catriona loved Sophy more dearly than any true sister might.

'What are you going to wear for the Social on Saturday evening?' Sophy asked, adding gloomily, 'I'm having to make over that blue serge I wore last winter! Oh, Catie! Don't you positively long for wonderful new dresses? Don't you wish you didn't have to wait until you're twenty-one to get your inheritance? I know *I* should!'

'I never think much about my inheritance,' Catriona replied truthfully. Her late father, Alexander Dunbar, had been a partner in a prosperous Liverpool firm of sugar refiners, and he and his wife had spent much of their married life overseas.

'To have some of the money would be very useful, of course,' she went on seriously, pushing at a heap of powdery snow with the snub toe of her boot. 'There are comforts I should like to give Granny that we simply can't afford — but there really isn't anything else I'd want to buy.'

'You haven't any imagination!' Sophy chided brightly. 'Now, when are you going to open Robbie's note? I'm dying to know what it says.' She peered around her friend's arm as Catriona began unfolding the thick paper.

'Oh, Catie — Hurry up!' cried Sophy in exasperation. 'What does Robbie say?'

'He wants me to meet him at the hollow log — '

Even as Catriona spoke, Sophy was holding on to her bonnet with one hand and using the other to raise her skirts clear of the snow as she darted away through the wood towards the loch.

Nevertheless, Catriona got to the hollow log first. Robert was already there, waiting for her. He heard her approaching and looked around, calling out and smiling broadly as he ran to meet her.

However, Robert's callow face revealed dismay when he saw Sophy Hamilton was following some three or four yards behind Catriona.

'Hello, Catriona,' he murmured. 'I'm glad you came — '

'You win, Catie!' panted Sophy, limping up to them, clutching her side. 'I'd have given you a closer race but for this wretched stitch!'

'Hello, Sophy,' Robert said absently, unable to take his eyes from Catriona's heart-shaped, pretty face. Her cheeks were rosy from the snowy afternoon and running, her eyes shining as she smiled up at him.

'I thought we might go skating. I brought my own skates.' Robert withdrew a mackintosh-wrapped bundle from within the hollow log. 'And I went to your grandmother's cottage and asked if I might have your skates, too. Annie fetched them for me.'

'What about mine?' exclaimed Sophy in dismay. 'How am I to skate?'

Robert flushed awkwardly. 'I'm sorry, Sophy. I just didn't think. If I'd realised you'd be here too, I would've brought yours also, of course.'

'Never mind,' Catriona said at once, turning to Sophy. 'We wear the same size. We can share my boots and take turns at skating.'

'Thanks, you're a plum!' Sophy beamed. 'You go first. I'll rest and catch my breath, until this stitch in my side goes.'

While the girls sat on the log, Robert laced the heavy brown skating boots on to Catriona's slender feet, before bashfully taking her gloved hand into his own and leading her onto the ice. Then, slowly drawing her away from Sophy's sight around the curving bank of the loch, Robert impulsively slipped his arms about Catriona's slim waist, lowering his lips to hers.

'Robert!' breathed Catriona, turning away. 'Don't — '

'Please, Catriona!' he mumbled thickly.

Catriona's pulse was suddenly racing as she felt the warmth of Robert's breath against her cold cheek, his mouth so urgently seeking her own, but she pushed him gently away from her.

Even as she slid from Robert's arms, skimming away across the shimmering frozen loch, Catriona's senses soared with the sweet, heady emotions his touch stirred within her.

⋆ ⋆ ⋆

Annie was bustling down the garden path as Catriona turned in to the gate with its trellised arch of evergreens.

'You're just in time, Miss Catriona!' Annie greeted her cheerfully. 'I've left tea laid and ready, all you need do is warm the pot!'

'Thank you, Annie.' Catriona smiled gratefully at the housekeeper, who'd been a treasure during Essie McPherson's illness. 'How's Granny?'

'Oh, she's no' so bad.' Annie nodded. 'Even a bit perkier, I'd say. She received a letter after you'd left for choir practice, so perhaps that has something to do with cheering her up!'

Essie McPherson was sitting in her rocking chair beside the fire in the snug, low-beamed parlour. She looked up and smiled as Catriona scurried indoors.

'Hurry and take off your things, and come over here, pet. We'll have our tea in front of the fire.' She patted the plump cushion beside her chair. 'I've some thrilling news for you . . . '

'Invited to Pelham?' Catriona exclaimed in astonishment some few

16

minutes later, when she was pouring the tea. 'I don't understand, Granny — we haven't heard from the Espleys in years!'

'Steady on, you'll have the tray over!' laughed Essie. 'However, you're correct. We did lose touch with them, which was quite wrong, because the Espleys are your only other relatives — and family *is* family, when all's said and done.

'But there, that's all put to rights now, because Samuel Espley — your father's cousin — has written inviting you to spend the whole season at Pelham!'

'A trip — all the way to Friars Quay in Lancashire!' Catriona shook her head in disbelief, sitting back on her heels before the glowing fire. 'I've never been on a trip before!'

'Then it's high time you did!' Essie said. 'You should get to know your cousins, too. Lucy, she's only a little older than you; and Julian, who must be about twenty-six by now. Perhaps he's even married with a family of his own.

'To be truthful,' she went on, 'I never did care much for Samuel Espley, and your father wasn't close to him either. Nonetheless, they were cousins, and family meant a great deal to Alexander.'

'What's Samuel Espley like?' asked Catriona, curious about this distant relative who was completely unknown to her.

Essie considered. 'Samuel's a brusque, rather domineering man. Accustomed to giving orders and having them immediately obeyed. He owns ships at Liverpool and has a flourishing company, so perhaps that accounts for his manner and sense of importance.

'By contrast, however, Samuel's wife is an absolute delight! Amanda's the most charming and kindliest woman. She cared for you as tenderly as she would her own child after your parents were lost with the *Rhiannon*.'

Catriona nodded. She'd been a wee

girl sailing from America with her parents when the *Rhiannon* struck a string of savage rocks on the Marram Shore, just a few short miles from her home harbour.

Rhiannon was one of Samuel Espley's own ships, heavily laden with cargo bound for Liverpool, and carrying less than a dozen passengers. Only a handful of survivors were rescued from the turbulent sea raging about the heaving, doomed wreck — Catriona had been amongst them.

Samuel Espley had claimed *Rhiannon* was deliberately wrecked by her captain. There'd been investigations and a trial. Captain Chappel was found guilty of the crime and imprisoned with a life sentence. Catriona had been told these things by Essie McPherson, but she hadn't any actual memory of the dreadful night *Rhiannon* had gone down, nor even of her brief stay at Pelham and being so gently cared for by Amanda Espley.

'Tell me about Pelham, Granny,' said

Catriona, hugging her knees. 'What is the house like?'

'I visited only once, but I remember Pelham as a simply beautiful place!' Essie recalled. 'Very grand and fashionable, mind. Filled with music and elegant furniture and fine paintings — your Aunt Amanda has exquisite taste. She's very accomplished, too. Amanda sketches and plays and sings.'

Catriona's hazel eyes were shining with excitement. 'When shall I set off?'

'Oh, as soon as can be arranged, I think.' Essie beamed. 'Fetch your grandpa's old map from the bureau, and we'll plot your journey down to Lancashire. Pelham lies right on the coast.'

Catriona rose from her cushion and crossed to the bureau by the window. As she rolled up the polished walnut lid, she glanced out across the village to the Mathieson house —

And the wonder of those fleeting moments at the loch, when Robert had tried to kiss her, flooded back . . .

3

It was a fine morning. Spring sunshine was melting the last of the lochside snows, and dancing across scattered drifts of wild flowers in Essie McPherson's wee cottage garden, as Catriona neatly placed the last of her belongings into the sturdy bag she was taking to Friars Quay.

Her trunk had already been stowed on to the box of the coach which would carry Catriona from Strathlachie and south as far as the Borders. She then had to change coach for the remainder of her journey.

'Nearly ready, pet?' Essie McPherson asked cheerfully, coming into Catriona's room. 'My, you do look bonny! And suddenly all grown up, going away on your first trip, and — ' She broke off in consternation as her granddaughter ran into her arms, just as she had when

21

she was a wee girl.

'Why, Catriona — whatever's this long sad face in aid of?'

'Oh, I shall miss you so much, Granny!' exclaimed Catriona, hugging her grandmother tightly. 'And Robert and Sophy, too!'

'Of course you will, and we'll miss you, pet,' Essie said sensibly as they went through to the parlour.

Crossing to the walnut bureau by the window, she took out a small, oval brooch. The amethysts glowed softly in the wintry sunlight, warm and precious in their setting of rich, old gold.

'This is for you, pet.'

'But, Granny!' breathed Catriona in astonishment. 'It's Mother's brooch — the one Papa gave her when they became betrothed!'

Essie gently pressed the amethyst brooch into Catriona's hands. 'Be sure to wear it in happiness, pet — ah, here's Sophy coming to say goodbye!'

Catriona followed her grandmother's gaze through the little window and saw

Sophy Hamilton hurrying up the path.

'I did think we'd be seeing Robert this morning,' ventured Essie tactfully, glancing around at Catriona. 'Is he not coming to see you off?'

'We've said our goodbyes, Granny,' she replied, hesitating slightly before adding, 'When I come back from Friars Quay, Robert wants us to be married.'

'And what do you want?' asked Essie softly.

Catriona met her grandmother's eyes steadily. 'I love him, Granny.'

'Then that's all that matters.' Essie smiled.

'Thank you, Granny!' Catriona gave her grandmother a final hug before answering Sophy's impatient knocking at the cottage door.

'Take care!' Essie McPherson called a little later, waving from the cottage doorstone as she watched Catriona climbing up into the coach. 'Come back to me soon, pet!'

★ ★ ★

Catriona was making the long journey unchaperoned, and as the days slipped by and the miles rattled away beneath the coach team's hooves, she soon became seasoned to travelling alone and fending for herself.

'Friars Quay!' the driver called, eventually turning the blowing horses into an inn yard.

Catriona alighted from the coach stiffly, stamping the cramp from her feet. There was no sign of her aunt or uncle, nor of any carriage from Pelham waiting to meet her.

'I'll put your goods over here, shall I, miss?' The driver smiled at her kindly, setting Catriona's luggage down next to a bench beside the coaching inn's side door, then turned away to clamber aboard the stagecoach once more. 'Good-day to you, miss!'

Catriona returned the driver's cheery farewell, watching the coach with its few remaining passengers trundle southwards to Liverpool, while she settled down on the bench to await the

Espleys' carriage.

A distant church clock struck the hour, and Catriona shifted uneasily. Where on earth was the carriage from Pelham?

The afternoon was already closing in, and although the actual coastline was not within sight, Catriona could certainly feel the cold mist rolling in off the sea. Its dampness was seeping through the layers of her clothing, chilling her to the marrow. She shivered, envying the blacksmith the heat of the blistering fire flaring within the open-sided forge at the far side of the inn's yard.

The glowing coals threw florid light up onto the smith's sweat-streaked face and burly arms as he pounded a huge white-hot iron shoe into shape on the sparking anvil. The smith occasionally half-turned to exchange comments with a tall, dark man whose face Catriona could not distinguish, for he stood away from the spitting fire in the gloom of the forge.

Whatever the reason responsible for the Espleys' carriage being so delayed, Catriona was unwilling to linger any longer in the gathering dusk. The few coins in her purse were all that was left of the small sum Essie McPherson had been able to spare Catriona for travelling expenses, and they certainly wouldn't be sufficient to hire a carriage and driver — even if these were available at such a poor establishment as Friars Quay Inn.

Which left only one alternative.

Taking hold of her bulky bag, Catriona strode purposefully along the yard and past the forge to the livery stable, where a young boy with a shaggy mongrel collie was forking fresh straw into the middle stall.

'Excuse me,' Catriona began quietly. 'Can you direct me to Pelham, please?'

'Reckon I know where it is, if that's what you mean, miss,' he replied with a cheeky grin, nodding in the direction of a broad, dusty track winding away from the inn. 'Go down that road there, and keep going till you get to the shore. Then you'll see Pelham. Great big house, it is. You can't miss it.

'But it's a fair few miles away,' the lad finished thoughtfully. 'You'll not make it afore dark, not if you're on foot.'

'I don't have much choice!' Catriona smiled wryly. 'Would you kindly ask the innkeeper if I may leave my trunk here, until someone from Pelham can fetch it for me?'

'No need to ask him, miss,' answered the lad cheerfully. 'Jack Lippitt won't mind. I'll see to it for you. My name's Huddy Unsworth, miss.'

'Well, thank you for your help, Huddy.'

Catriona considered the stable boy a moment. He could be no older than eight or nine. Impulsively, she reached into her purse and took out two of the coins, pressing them into Huddy Unsworth's cold, grimy hand.

'Thanks, miss!' His face lit up, scarcely able to believe his unexpected wealth as he turned the coins over and over between his fingers.

Catriona started onto the beach road, but after a moment, Huddy sprinted after her, his dog bounding along beside him.

'Miss! Miss!' He caught her up, the excited brown collie capering around the boy's bony ankles. 'See that bloke in the smithy there? He's Morgan — hired hand out at Pelham. Wait here while I tell him.' Huddy was already turning back towards the forge. 'Happen he'll drive you down there!'

Even in the dull nether light betwixt day and night, Catriona could not mistake the frown upon the broad-shouldered man's face as he strode unhurriedly across the inn yard towards her.

'I'm Morgan, miss. The Espleys' hired man.' He raised his faded, wide-brimmed hat politely, and Catriona saw his strong hands were lean and calloused from hard, unremitting labour. The skin of his hands and face was dark, tanned by sea and wind and the harsh weathers of this cragged coast; yet Morgan clearly was not local-born, for Catriona recognised distinct traces of a soft Welsh lilt in his low voice.

'The lad tells me you're bound for Pelham, miss?'

'Yes. I arrived with the afternoon coach. The Espleys are expecting me, and I believed their carriage would meet me,' Catriona explained briefly. 'As you can see, it has not done so. I was about to begin walking to Pelham; however, Huddy warns me the house is some distance away.'

'That it is, miss,' Morgan commented evenly. There was an uncanny, almost luminous blueness to his eyes that Catriona had noticed immediately. His steady gaze was not for a moment leaving her face, and while his tone gave away nothing of his thoughts, Catriona could see from his eyes he disbelieved her story.

'So the Espleys are expecting you, miss?'

'They are,' returned Catriona irritably. She was cold and exhausted and in no mood to have her word doubted. 'Can you drive me out to Pelham or not?'

'I could do that,' he remarked, without making any movement. 'However, the Master is away from Pelham at present, and Mister Julian is out and likely won't be back this side of morning. There's nobody there at the house, miss.'

'This doesn't make any sense!' exclaimed Catriona in exasperation. 'I tell you, I'm *expected* at Pelham! The Espleys are my late father's cousins. I'm Catriona Dunbar — '

'Dunbar?' echoed Morgan sharply, his clear blue eyes glinting in the half-light and drilling into her.

'You recognise the name?' queried Catriona, flinching uncomfortably beneath his penetrating stare.

Morgan shrugged. 'I heard it once, miss,' he replied carelessly. 'A long time ago.'

Turning away from her, Morgan started with easy, measured strides across the murky yard. 'Soon as the horse is ready, we'll get on our way, miss.'

Morgan duly harnessed the horse between the shafts of the heavy waggon, loading Catriona's heavy trunk into the waggon-bed.

'My apologies for not bringing the carriage, miss,' he said, helping Catriona up on to the rough, wooden seat. 'I wasn't given orders to meet the coach today.'

'I simply can't understand it!' Catriona reasoned, as Morgan climbed up into the seat beside her. 'It is at Uncle Samuel's own invitation I am here at all!'

'Happen the Master confused the date you were arriving, miss,' Morgan commented, lacing the worn reins through his long fingers. 'Since the accident, the Master's not always . . . *well*.'

'Accident?' echoed Catriona. 'What

accident might this be?'

'It's years past, miss. I was still a boy, but I remember it happening well enough,' Morgan returned evenly. 'The Master was out diving. The current caught him and swept him onto the rocks. He was badly crushed.'

Catriona shook her head sadly. 'I had no idea.'

'Like I say, miss. It's years past. The Master's able to get about fair enough now.'

'You said there was no one at Pelham this evening,' began Catriona after a few moments elapsed. She was feeling increasingly perplexed by the whole situation. 'But what of Mrs Espley — my Aunt Amanda — and Cousin Lucy? Are they away from home, too?'

'Like I said, miss,' answered Morgan quietly, 'there's nobody at Pelham tonight.'

The waggon lurched, bouncing over a hummocky rise, and suddenly the ocean lay before Catriona; its curling, white-ragged waves rising and rolling up the deserted shore, thumping softer than a sigh against algae-strewn rocks that gleamed silvery in the cold moonshine.

Catriona caught her breath, awed by the spectacular beauty of rippling sea and starry sky.

'First time at the coast, miss?' Morgan asked, watching her response to the seascape stretching before them.

'The first time I recall,' Catriona answered, inhaling deeply the tangy salt air. 'I was at Pelham for a while when I was a wee girl, but I don't remember anything about that visit. Not even the sea!' she enthused excitedly. 'Oh, Morgan — it's magnificent!'

'Aye, she's beguiling and gentle as a lover tonight,' admitted Morgan, his even white teeth flashing in an amiable grin. 'You just wait until she's wild and angry and jealous. No matter how hard you may try, you'll not be able to shut out from your ears the roar of the tide, nor the howling north-westerlies that drive her.'

'I'm sure I shall adore the sea, whatever her mood!' laughed Catriona.

Morgan raised a dark eyebrow. 'The sea's like a fever, miss,' he went on, and although his tone was still carefree, Catriona saw the humour fading from his eyes. 'Once she's in your blood, you're bewitched, and never can be free of her again.'

'That's a strange thing to say — ' began Catriona is surprise; however, even as she spoke, they reached a fork in the sandy track. Morgan turned the waggon away from the beach into a dark avenue of still-naked sycamore and elm, looming twisted and skeletal against the sky and casting deep, distorted shadows across their path.

'Must we continue on just yet?' she enquired, craning her neck to glance back to the seashore. 'I'd like to watch the sea coming in a little while longer!'

'Low tide tonight, miss.' Morgan spoke almost as though thinking aloud. 'Nothing happens on a quiet night like this . . . ' Jumping down from the waggon, he opened the tall, ornately-wrought iron gates into Pelham.

A tall house reared up before them from dense shadow. Catriona gasped. She had never seen a more sombre, less welcoming sight!

'This is Pelham.' Morgan's voice was uncharacteristically harsh. 'Home and haunt of the illustrious Espleys.'

Morgan drove the waggon through an archway and around to the rear of the house. Instantly, they were bathed in the almost supernatural light of moon and sea, and Catriona saw that Pelham's gardens sloped straight downwards to the shorefields. Morgan drew the waggon close to a huge laurel hedge sprawling unchecked against the stone blocks of the wall, almost covering the narrow mullioned windows of washhouse and kitchen.

'I don't know what I'm to do with you, miss,' Morgan said, opening the low kitchen door and respectfully bidding Catriona enter. 'The maidservant Eliza will be long gone home to the village. And what with Mister Julian and the Master both being out, Hannah — she's the housekeeper — took the chance to slip away and visit her brother over at Sandford.'

Morgan lit the thick stump of candle standing on the mantel, and bent to throw more kindling onto the dying fire, raking it until the dry logs caught and flared.

'There's nobody here to attend to you, miss. Nobody here at all, but thee and me.'

'That's alright, Morgan. I can take care of myself,' Catriona replied, drawn close to the hearth by the warmth from the fire. She stood next to Morgan, stretching out her cold hands gratefully to the heat from the glowing logs.

'Happen there's soup or suchlike on the stove or somewhere,' Morgan began, glancing around the kitchen awkwardly. 'Hannah usually leaves something for whenever Mister Julian gets back.'

Catriona frowned into the crackling

blaze. There was nothing else to do but make the best of her dilemma. She had warmth and shelter, and would find the makings of a simple supper. If need be, she could sleep on the oak settle here in the kitchen.

Morgan brought in her trunk from the waggon, setting it down onto the stone-flagged floor.

'Will there be anything else, miss?'

'Erm, no. Thank you, Morgan,' replied Catriona, hesitating as to whether it would be proper to invite him to share some hot tea with her.

'I shall get off then, miss,' he said, taking his hat from where he'd left it on the wood box. 'If you should need anything, my room's just yonder. The hayloft over the stables — '

Morgan broke off as light footsteps tripped quickly down the back stairs towards the kitchen.

Catriona glanced at him quickly. 'You said there wasn't anyone else here?'

'Happen there shouldn't be, miss,' remarked Morgan drily, but Catriona observed he wasn't in the least surprised when a mousy-haired girl of about sixteen burst excitedly into the kitchen. Stopping abruptly in her tracks, the eager smile instantly disappeared from her elfin face when she confronted Catriona and Morgan standing there.

'I reckon we're not who you were expecting to see, eh, Eliza?' Morgan half-grinned at the maidservant. 'Well, since you're still here, happen you'll take care of Miss Catriona. She's the Master's guest.'

'The Master's guest?' Eliza repeated curtly. 'I wasn't told to expect any guest, and besides, I should've gone home hours ago!'

'Then why are you still here?' declared Morgan bitterly. 'As if I needed to ask!'

He unlatched the door, and cold salt air rushed into the kitchen.

'Goodnight. miss,' Morgan paused on the threshold, casting a scathing glance at the sullen maidservant. 'You'd best show Miss Catriona to her room, Eliza.'

Eliza's attention returned to Catriona, her pale eyes narrowing suspiciously.

'Was Morgan telling me right? Are you really the *Master's* guest?'

Catriona didn't begin to comprehend the emphasis Eliza placed upon the question, but she nodded wearily.

'My father and Mr Samuel Espley were cousins.'

'So you're kin, then?' exclaimed Eliza, the tension leaving her voice. 'Sort of a cousin yourself, like? To the Master's son and daughter, that is?'

'I suppose.'

'Right, then.' Eliza began to bustle efficiently about the kitchen, laying plates and cutlery upon the bare table, and fetching a tray of cold pie, bread, cheese, and slicing onions from the pantry.

'Hannah — she's the housekeeper, miss — didn't say you were coming, so I've no room ready for you. Anyhow, you get on and eat your supper while I light the fire in Miss Lucy's old room and put a few hot bricks into the bed, all ready for when you go up.'

That night, in spite of her weariness, Catriona lay wakeful. The air within the room was stale. The acrid smell of dust and mildew clung to the drapes and linen, and Catriona had the distinct impression this evidently once-comfortable room had been shuttered and unused; forgotten, almost, for a very long while.

Catriona had placed the precious amethyst brooch upon the dressing-table, where she could see it as she lay huddled in the large, cold bed.

Long-ago fond memories of her grandmother, of home in Strathlachie, of her dear friends — and especially of Robert — crowded in upon Catriona's over-tired mind. Everything she cared about seemed so hopelessly far away and beyond her reach.

Catriona shivered, closing her eyes tightly to shut out the homesickness and the damp chill. Finally cocooning the counterpane about her shoulders and creeping from the bed to the hearth, she curled up, willing sleep to come.

But during that long first night at Pelham, her thoughts of Robert Mathieson were all that warmed Catriona's cold and lonely heart.

4

Catriona awakened stiff and chilled to the bone the following morning. Cold, grey daylight was seeping into the room, and with a start Catriona realised that, despite everything, she'd slept much later than usual.

Lying still for a moment, she could hear the normal household sounds of somebody moving about downstairs: doors opening and closing, the clattering of pans and plates.

Catriona rose, washed in the cold water from the pitcher, and dressed quickly in her warmest clothes. Her fingertips lingered fondly upon the amethyst brooch as she pinned it securely at the neck of her sturdy homespun bodice.

Her room must be almost directly above the kitchen, because down below were the cobbled yard and stables, and the age-greened stone archway through which the waggon had entered. Morgan was down in the yard, bent over the wood-chopping block as he skilfully hewed a new spoke for one of the waggon's large wheels, which stood propped at his side. Catriona watched him idly, twisting her hair into thick braids. However, she quickly stepped back from sight as Eliza emerged from the blackthorn patch which wound around from the side of the stables.

A broad grin spread across Eliza's pert face when she spotted Morgan. Leaving the earth path, her footsteps rang quick and light upon the cobbles, and Morgan glanced up at her jaunty approach.

Catriona couldn't hear the words the pair exchanged, but she saw Eliza start to laugh, swinging her full hips so she nudged against Morgan's shoulder as he bent once more to his work. With a final, bantering quip, the maid ruffled Morgan's shock of blue-black hair and sauntered on towards the house.

Catriona guessed they must be sweethearts, and with an earnest wish to be back together with her own sweetheart in Strathlachie, she fleetingly appraised her reflection in the glass before going downstairs.

At the foot of the wide, turned staircase, rooms opened off upon either side. Catriona could hear activity, and smell bread baking, so wandered down a narrow passageway until she came to the kitchen door, beyond which two women were gossiping.

'I don't remember her name exactly — something queer, it was — ' Eliza was saying, her frown breaking into a wide grin as she paused from turning the heavy handle of the churn. 'Honest, Hannah, when I first come down and saw her standing here with her bag and bundles, I reckoned she must be one of Mister Julian's young ladies come looking for him!'

'Mind your tongue, Eliza!' the housekeeper snapped sharply. 'It's not for the likes of you to tittle-tattle about your betters!'

'I was only saying what I thought!' retorted Eliza obstinately.

'Well, don't,' Hannah cautioned, banging another batch of bread dough onto the table. 'If the Master catches you talking that way, there'll be trouble!'

'I'm not frightened of the old man,' declared Eliza airily, pulling a ribbon from her mousy hair and retying it with a flourish. 'Nor the young one, neither!'

'One of these days, you'll learn your lesson the hard way, my girl!' Hannah commented, eyeing the young maid critically. 'There's them, and there's us. You'd best remember it and get on with your work. That milk won't churn itself into butter!'

Seconds later, Eliza was approaching the door, and Catriona was flustered. She was embarrassed and vexed by what she'd overheard, but wasn't ready to confront the two women in their own kitchen, particularly the dour house-keeper. Darting away from the kitchen door, Catriona's seeking hand found the smooth brass knob of a room across the hall. Hurriedly letting herself inside, she closed the door soundlessly.

At once, Catriona realised she was not alone.

In the gloom of the heavily-shuttered drawing-room, a thick-set man was slumped in a high-backed chair close to the fire, his breathing noisy as he slept.

'Ah, so you're in here, are you, miss?'

Catriona whirled around as the door opened briskly and Eliza strode in.

'We was wondering when you'd come down,' the maid went on chirpily, stepping over the man's sprawled feet to stoke up the fire. 'Hannah said best to let you sleep as long as you wanted. After your long journey and all. Are you hungry?'

Catriona nodded. 'Yes. Very.'

'No need to whisper, miss.' Eliza grinned, cocking her head to the slumbering man. 'He'll not hear you — '

From somewhere at the front of the old house, a heavy door slammed and loud footfalls echoed along the hall.

'Eliza!' The voice was impatient.

'Coming, sir!' She trotted to the doorway as a tall, strong-jawed man in his middle twenties strode in. 'You wanted me, Mister Julian?'

'You'll have to do. Actually, I wanted our noble hired hand.' Julian Espley's forehead creased into an irritated frown. 'Find him, Eliza,' he went on, stripping off his sand-flecked outdoor garments and tossing them to the maid. 'Tell him Bartie Ashmoore and I are taking on the Loxwoods across country this afternoon. Morgan's to have my horses ready by one o'clock.'

'Yes, sir.' Eliza bobbed an awkward curtsey and scuttled from the drawing-room.

Julian threw himself into one of the chairs, and fixed his attention onto

Catriona, as though only now noticing her presence.

'Who are you? Surely Hannah hasn't finally wheedled herself a new scullery maid!' demanded Julian wryly. 'Well, don't just stand there, girl — take off my boots!'

'I certainly will not!' she returned indignantly. 'Take them off yourself!'

To Catriona's astonishment, Julian threw back his head and laughed heartily at her.

'Your voice gives you away, miss! You must be none other than Cousin Catriona!' he exclaimed. 'I was aware Father had written to your grandmother, but not that he had invited you to come so soon. How old are you?'

Catriona bridled slightly. 'Fifteen — almost sixteen.'

'You don't look it,' he observed, appraising her dispassionately. 'Still, you have pretty eyes. And your hair's a handsome enough colour. Your sort often develop into unexpected beauties and so confound even your harshest critics.'

'Do you sum up everyone you meet as if they were horseflesh?' retorted Catriona crossly.

Julian pulled an amused face, rubbing his chin as though seriously considering. 'Actually, I suppose I do. Well, *women*, at least!'

He jumped to his feet, snapping his heels together and half-bowing. 'Julian Espley. Your servant, Miss Dunbar! Only son and heir to all you see before and around you — may heaven help me!'

Waving vaguely in the direction of the slumbering man, he went on. 'That recumbent fellow in his cups is, of course, your Uncle Samuel, Master of Pelham and owner of the once-renowned Espley Shipping Line of Liverpool!'

Julian was prowling around the dimly-lit room now, peering on shelves and under tables before triumphantly raising a decanter from beside the fire dogs.

'Ah, splendid! Father hasn't quite drained the cellar dry.' Taking the crystal decanter by the neck, Julian winked at Catriona conspiratorially before making for the door. 'Purely for medicinal purposes, so I might revitalise my strengths for the rigours of the Loxwoods' race this afternoon . . .'

Catriona stood perplexed after he'd gone, deliberating upon what to do next, when Samuel Espley suddenly rallied.

He groaned horribly, opening pallid eyes and fixing Catriona's face with a rheumy, unfocussed stare. His hand reached out and clutched at Catriona's skirts. She pulled away in panic, her feet skidding and stumbling over a walking cane lying carelessly on the floor. And with Julian Espley's ramblings still loud in her ears, Catriona fled from the drawing-room, up the stairs and into her own room. Slamming the door behind her, she turned the great key and locked it fast.

Grabbing her bag, Catriona's trembling hands fumbled with the bindings as she hastily gathered her few belongings and stuffed them inside.

She couldn't stay in this awful place a moment longer. She'd go home. To her grandmother. To Robert —

Catriona froze, a shudder of stark realisation overtaking her. How *could* she return to Strathlachie? Her purse was almost empty! Essie McPherson had scrimped together all of her meagre savings simply to send Catriona to Friars Quay . . .

Giving her granddaughter this trip to Pelham had meant so much to Essie, and Catriona did not have the heart to hurt the old lady by telling her the Espley house and family were no longer as she remembered them!

No, decided Catriona, wandering to the window and staring bleakly down to the seashore. She had no choice but remain at Pelham and make the best of things.

★　★　★

Washing her flushed face in the cold water, Catriona tidied her hair before going downstairs again.

Taking a deep breath, she straightened her shoulders and went into the kitchen before courage failed her.

'Good morning,' she said politely, greatly relieved to find the middle-aged housekeeper alone. 'May I have something to eat, please?'

Hannah threw her a sour glance. 'While you're here, you'll eat in the kitchen with us,' she said, pointedly leaving off her pastry-making to fetch a cup and plate from the dresser. 'Dining-room's not used no more, except on occasion when the Master's fit.

'Eliza and me are too busy to fuss with a child,' the housekeeper concluded. 'You'll not be waited on as you're likely used to.'

'I'm not a child. And I'm *not* accustomed to being waited upon, Mrs — Hannah,' stressed Catriona earnestly. There was a firmness to her soft voice that caught the housekeeper's keen attention. 'I can cook, and I'm used to doing chores. I'll be glad to help — '

An almighty crash from across the hall had Hannah pushing past Catriona and out of the kitchen. She burst into the drawing-room, with Catriona at her heels.

Catriona's hand flew to her mouth in horror at the sight she observed.

Samuel Espley was sprawled upon the floor, floundering and crying out as though in some fevered delirium.

'Amanda . . . *Amanda!*' he moaned over and over, his upturned face staring at Hannah.

But his eyes were blank and expressionless. Catriona realised her uncle really wasn't aware of herself or Hannah at all.

'There, there, Master.' Hannah's voice was uncharacteristically gentle. 'You've taken a nasty fall, that's all. Open the shutters, miss!' she ordered. 'Let's get some light in!'

53

Catriona obediently pulled back the heavy curtains and unlatched the panelled wooden shutters.

When daylight flooded the gloomy drawing-room, Catriona saw her uncle clearly for the first time. It was obvious to her that Samuel Espley had not shaved nor changed his clothing for several days, for he was dishevelled and unkempt: his greying hair disarrayed and caked with mud, his shirt and waistcoat badly soiled and stained with liquor and soil.

To Catriona's horror, her uncle suddenly burst into anguished, racking sobs, and tears spilled down his face leaving tracks in the grime on his veined cheeks.

'Take no notice, miss. It's just the drink,' Hannah said matter-of-factly, cradling Samuel's head. 'His grieving was done long ago.'

'He's gashed his face.' Catriona's throat was tight. She could hardly get the words out. 'I'll fetch some water to bathe the cut.'

* * *

'You did right well in there, miss,' Hannah remarked when she and Catriona were back in the kitchen together. The housekeeper considered Catriona's pinched, white face. 'Best sit yourself down by the fire, lass. You look exhausted. I'll brew a fresh pot of tea.'

Catriona sat in the chimney corner. Now the incident with Uncle Samuel was over, she couldn't stop shaking, and gratefully cupped the mug of hot, sweet tea in her cold hands.

'Is he always like that?'

Hannah sighed heavily. 'The Master has bad spells, miss,' she replied, setting a plate of piping hot buttered crumpets beside Catriona. 'Weeks'll go by and he won't set foot from the house. He just stays in that room and drinks.

'Other times, he'll be sober as a bishop. Gets spruced up and drives off in the carriage, and we'll not see him for days on end. He comes back like you saw him,' she finished, sitting across the hearth from Catriona. 'Drunk. His money all gone on liquor and gambling.'

Catriona sipped the scalding-hot tea slowly, trying to understand. 'My uncle was calling for Amanda, and you said his grieving was over long ago,' she began. 'Is my aunt dead, Hannah?'

'Amanda Espley's alive, miss,' the housekeeper replied simply. 'But she's lost to the Master for good and all.'

'Where is she? And Cousin Lucy too?'

'Gone. One day the mistress just upped and left. Went back to her parents in Grassendale, and took little Miss Lucy with her,' Hannah related gravely. 'It was them going that finally broke him.'

'You're fond of my uncle, aren't you?' Catriona murmured tentatively.

'Aye, miss. Reckon I am,' Hannah admitted ruefully. 'I'm a fool to myself, because he treats me as bad as he treats everybody else. But you see, I remember him as he *used* to be.'

'Before my aunt and cousin left?'

'Nay, many a long year before that!' Hannah smiled sadly. 'When I were a slip of a lass no older than you, Samuel Espley was young and handsome, and he'd made a fortune from shipping cotton and spices and suchlike. He was a fine figure of a man! Active and powerful. And him and your aunt were like newly-weds, even after the bairns came along — ' Hannah's voice dropped to a whisper.

'Master and Julian were out sailing, but summat happened. An accident. I'm not sure what exactly. Anyhow, young Julian brought him ashore single-handed. Your uncle's body was all twisted and broken. I'll never forget that night! A man such as him would rather be in his grave than crippled the way he is now. He's lost interest in everything and everybody.'

'Poor Uncle!' Catriona was suddenly ashamed of how harshly she'd judged him. 'Was that when Aunt Amanda and Lucy left Pelham?'

'Oh, bless you, no, miss!' replied Hannah in surprise. 'If anything, your aunt loved him all the more. I never heard so much as a cross word between them. One evening they'd been to a ball over at Larks Grange. Came home in high old spirits! Laughing and talking just like they always did. The Master's valet was getting him into bed, and Amanda went into the drawing-room to put her jewels back in the safe.

'Next morning, she'd gone. And she'd taken Lucy with her,' concluded Hannah with a resigned shake of her head. 'Don't ask me why, miss, because I don't know!'

After their curious conversation, Catriona spent the remainder of the day exploring the desolate rooms of Pelham.

The rambling mansion was sadly run-down and in dire need of thorough refurbishment. The dining-room still contained some exquisite furniture, and the library was a fine one, although it pained Catriona to see so many

58

beautiful books neglected to dust and mildew.

She gathered a posy of wild flowers from the overgrown gardens and took them up to her room. Their fresh colours seemed to radiate life and brightness, and Catriona was arranging the late daffodils, primroses and blue-bells upon her dressing-table when Hannah popped her head around the door.

'The Master's up and about — ' The housekeeper looked harassed. 'Dinner's in an hour, miss. And you're to dress.'

Catriona put on her best Sunday floral and duly went downstairs. Her doubts about the suitability of her dress were no greater than her apprehension at what her uncle's present condition might be.

Hesitantly entering the drawing-room, Catriona was dumbfounded by the transformation so few hours had wrought in Samuel Espley!

Dressed immaculately for dinner, this distinguished gentleman gallantly rose to his feet, depending heavily upon two canes as he stepped forward to greet her cordially.

'Catriona, welcome to Pelham! Do join us,' Samuel began, adding apologetically, 'Please forgive my not meeting you from the coach last evening — unfortunately, pressing business detained me in Liverpool.'

'Would that have been the grape or the grain?' Julian enquired with a crooked smile. 'No, not even *you* can subdue my spirits this evening, dear Papa!' he laughed, shrugging off his father's glance of grim disapproval. 'Bartie Ashmoore and I soundly out-rode and out-raced those dullard Loxwood brothers this afternoon — and won a fine purse for our victory!'

'Judge Loxwood and his family are friends and neighbours of ours, Catriona,' explained Samuel genially, but the pulse beating at his temple betrayed his annoyance. 'They live at Larks Grange, several miles inland. Maud Loxwood is a fine young woman.

Perhaps my son will one day have sufficiently good manners to drive you over to meet her.

'Now — ' Leaning awkwardly on the canes, Samuel Espley offered Catriona his arm. 'Shall we go in to dinner, my dear Catriona?'

Despite the amicable dinner-table atmosphere her uncle strove to create, Catriona sensed the undercurrent of hostility between Samuel and his son, and she was relieved when finally she was able to retire and leave the men to their port and cigars.

Hours later, when Pelham was silent, Catriona sat in bed reading a book of poetry she'd brought up from the library. However, her choice had been a mistake, for reading the romantic verse made Catriona miss Robert all the more, and her longing for him was all the keener.

Slipping from her room, she tiptoed down to the drawing-room in search of writing materials. Even writing a letter to Robert would bring him nearer for a while!

Rolling up the lid of the bureau, Catriona quickly found pen and note-paper amongst the cluttered contents; however, as she searched for ink, a crumpled pile of papers slithered from a pigeon-hole onto the floor.

Catriona bent to retrieve them. She didn't mean to pry, but couldn't help seeing these were all overdue accounts from tailor, chandler, grocer . . . all manner of tradesmen and merchants.

Replacing the papers neatly, Catriona hurried back to her room to begin Robert's letter, never giving the creditors' notes another thought.

5

In that house, not a day passed without acrimonious rows erupting between father and son. What disturbed Catriona most was that Samuel and Julian appeared to relish the quarrels and take perverse satisfaction from taunting each other.

Catriona would have returned home immediately, had this been possible. Only Robert's letters were making the long weeks at Pelham bearable. The weather was generally warm and fine now, and each day Catriona gladly escaped from the house to wander for hours along the beach, or sought refuge in Hannah's kitchen.

Early one misty morning, Catriona was curled up in the chimney corner with her book when Morgan came into the kitchen for breakfast. Catriona knew he'd already been up to the village, and she glanced at him hopefully.

'Mail coach is delayed.' He smiled across at her, answering her silent question. 'Won't be in 'til noon tomorrow.'

'Sit yourself down, lad,' Hannah instructed. 'Eliza! Fetch his breakfast!'

'Morgan's one for book-reading too, miss,' commented Eliza, swishing close by where Catriona sat. 'Once upon a time, he wanted to be a lawyer or some such. Just fancy that!'

'Just fancy you getting on with your chores for once!' Hannah reprimanded sharply. 'Tea'll be mashed.'

Eliza banged a plate of hot muffins onto the table and poured Morgan's strong tea.

'This is the life!' he grinned. 'Waited on hand and foot!'

'Better make the most of it while you can,' she retorted tartly. 'I don't plan on being a maid much longer, y'know!'

Eliza was always giving Morgan the sharp edge of her tongue, but she giggled and flirted with him, too.

Catriona imagined they must meet secretly somewhere away from Pelham; for, after Eliza finished work, she often primped and preened in front of the glass before slipping away into the dark evening.

'You've dawdled long enough,' Hannah commented without turning from the stove to look at the flighty young maid. 'Hall's waiting to be bottomed.'

Eliza pulled a face behind the housekeeper's back and flounced from the kitchen.

Morgan had barely touched a mouthful of his meal when the door was flung open and Julian stood framed by the threshold, his pale eyes angry.

'Morgan, I might've guessed to find you in here gossiping like an old woman!' he said irritably. 'Redbird's waiting to be rubbed down. Damn beast threw a shoe coming down the spinney. Well, don't just sit there, man! Get to it — I'll want Redbird this evening!'

Catriona kept her eyes fixed upon her book, but she felt her face burning with discomfort.

Morgan instantly rose from the table and went out into the yard. Julian pulled off his gauntlets and strode across the kitchen towards the hall.

'I shall be attending the theatre this evening,' he remarked to Hannah, much of the annoyance gone from his voice. 'Be sure Eliza has my clothes ready in good time!'

While Hannah was busy in the pantry, Catriona laid aside her book, quietly poured a fresh mug of tea, and took it with Morgan's breakfast out to the stables.

'Miss?' He looked up questioningly as she pushed open the door.

'You haven't touched your breakfast. I brought it out for you,' she began shyly. 'I'm afraid the food's gone cold, but I made fresh tea.'

'That was thoughtful of you, miss. Thanks.'

He was carefully rubbing down the

sweating bay mare, and Catriona noticed flecks of dark blood on Redbird's fetlock.

'Is the horse hurt?' she asked in concern, stroking the bay's neck gently.

'Split hoof. Cuts and scratches,' answered Morgan tersely. 'She shouldn't have been ridden after she cast the shoe.'

'Julian rode her when she was lame?' Catriona exclaimed in disbelief. 'But I thought he was a good horseman!'

'So he is, miss. Likely the best in the whole county.' Morgan's quiet voice had a hard edge. 'But when there's a race or a wager to be won, Mister Julian rides like the devil. He lets nothing stand in his way.'

Catriona sat back on her heels in the clean straw, watching Morgan as he tended to the injured mare. 'Why do they fight all the while?' she ventured at length. 'My uncle, and Julian?'

'Too much of the same kind,' Morgan returned simply.

'The same kind?'

'Aye, and no amount of fighting can

ever change *that*!'

'I'm sorry for Uncle,' Catriona murmured sombrely. 'But I don't like him a bit. I've tried, and I just can't. And although it's scary when Uncle Samuel flies into one of his rages,' she confided dismally, 'there's something about Julian that *really* frightens me!'

Morgan watched her a while, sitting there in the straw with her small hands folded into her lap, her head bowed.

'We've a new foal, miss . . . ' began Morgan kindly. 'Would you like to feed him?'

'Oh, he's beautiful!' whispered Catriona in delight when the foal was nuzzling his velvety nose into her hand.

'Morgan,' she went on tentatively, for she was aware that servants generally didn't have reading or writing, 'when Eliza said you enjoyed reading books, was she speaking truthfully?'

'I like books well enough,' he replied guardedly. 'I inherit that from my mother. She'd read aloud to my sister and I, and to Pa, too, when he was ashore.'

'Does your family live here, in Friars Quay?'

'I lost my mother and sister to the influenza epidemic,' he answered after a moment. 'If my father had his choice, he would be dead, too.'

'Whatever do you mean?' Catriona was unable to conceal her shocked response.

'Pa's in gaol,' Morgan returned bitterly. 'And there he'll remain until the day he dies!'

'I'm so sorry, Morgan!' Catriona mumbled awkwardly, reaching out her hand to touch his arm. 'It must be awful for you.'

'Worse for him, miss,' Morgan responded, and Catriona saw clearly the pain and the anger within the depths of his earnest blue eyes. 'My father's an innocent man — serving sentence for another man's crime!'

* * *

'I have neither time nor inclination for playing nursemaid to a child!'

Julian's irate voice carried through the open windows of the drawing-room and out on the hot, still air to the garden where Catriona was clearing weeds from a sorely neglected flower bed.

'Your cousin is not a child!' Samuel Espley's words were slurred. He'd been drinking heavily for almost forty-eight hours. 'If you must go to the opera with Ashmoore and his wife, why not take Catriona and Maud Loxwood with you?'

'Because I choose not to!'

'You're a fool, Julian!' railed Samuel. 'Wasting your time hacking about with the Ashmoores! Bartie Ashmoore is a witless nincompoop!'

'Bartie happens to be my closest friend, and a distinguished Member of Parliament to boot!' Julian returned, adding scathingly, 'I find political affairs stimulating. You doubtless won't appreciate that, since you locate your own stimulation in the bottom of a glass!'

'You'd be better employed paying some attentions to Maud Loxwood,' spat Samuel. 'Why don't you marry her and be done with it?'

'And make your life easy?' demanded Julian in sarcastic incredulity. 'You won't turn Pelham and Espley Shipping over to my control, so why should I get you off the hook upon which your colossal incompetence has impaled you?

'Yes, I *will* marry Maud Loxwood,' he concluded savagely. 'When it suits my purposes — but not a day earlier!'

'If you're not a sight more careful, you'll lose her!'

Vainly trying to shut out the vicious argument between father and son, Catriona hurriedly finished her gardening and took the curving path down to the beach.

Stripping off her shoes and stockings, Catriona wandered along the deserted beach farther than she'd ever gone before, and presently came within sight of a tumbledown boathouse, tucked into a cove and sheltered by the high shelf of dunes and rocks rising behind and around it.

'Morgan!' Catriona shouted, hailing the hired hand as he strode down through the dunes towards the boathouse. 'I didn't know you had a boat!' she exclaimed breathlessly, running to meet him.

'It's not mine, miss. It belongs to Pelham,' he replied awkwardly, opening up the boathouse to reveal a small, well-maintained craft. 'But nobody at the house has sailed it for years. They've forgotten all about her, but I've been keeping her trim and seaworthy.'

Catriona glanced out at the soft waves, lapping beguilingly nearer. 'Are you going sailing today?'

'Aye, just for a short while,' he replied, dragging the boat down the hard sand. 'That hazy mist will likely roll into shore as fog before the afternoon's out.'

'Take me with you!' cried Catriona

impulsively, her eyes bright with excitement. 'Please, Morgan! I've never been sailing!'

Morgan considered doubtfully, before nodding slowly. 'Very well, miss.'

He eased the boat into the shallows and lifted Catriona aboard before pushing the vessel into deeper water and clambering aboard himself, taking the oars and rowing with smooth, even strokes.

'It's like being inside a picture!' Catriona exclaimed with delight, viewing the coastline as it gradually receded. 'There's Pelham — how different everything appears from out here! And surely that's the queer crooked chimney of the coaching inn, just visible between those hills?'

'Aye, it is. See over there, on that hilltop — ' He pointed to a grassy rise where a solitary, squat cottage sat back amongst a dense thicket of straggling, evergreen bushes. ' — that's Gorse Cottage. I lived there with my family.

And south of it, where that high point of land juts out to sea like a man's arm? That's Beacon Point. If the fog comes down thick, you'll likely see the beacon torches start burning.'

'To keep ships off the rocks, you mean?' Catriona queried with interest, breaking off as realisation dawned upon her. 'I hadn't even *thought*, Morgan! Isn't that dreadful? The ship my parents drowned upon must have gone down somewhere near here!'

'Aye, miss,' replied Morgan ruefully. 'She did. Way up yonder. On the Marram Shore.'

'You know about the *Rhiannon*?' exclaimed Catriona in surprise.

'My sister, mother and I were watching her coming in from the window of our cottage,' he said solemnly. 'I left them indoors and ran outside. I was on the beach when the *Rhiannon* foundered over the Combs. That's a drawn-out string of perilous rocks, miss.'

'You saw the wreck?' Her throat was tight.

'I did, miss,' he answered softly. '*Rhiannon* was a sturdy old ship, but she didn't have a chance once she hit the Combs. Neither did most of the good folk aboard.'

As Morgan rowed further out, swirls of damp mist gradually absorbed their small boat, and although they were now quite near a brig at anchor, Catriona could barely make out the ship's tall mast and motionless sails through the shifting haze.

'She's like a wraith — not a proper ship at all!'

'Oh, she's real, right enough — it's the *Candeloro*.' murmured Morgan grimly.

'I saw her — the *Candeloro* — from the beach,' went on Catriona, intrigued by the misty, romantic vision before her eyes. 'Is she waiting for the wind and the tide?'

'She's waiting all right, miss,' Morgan commented soberly. 'But not for wind nor tide. If I guess right, by morning she'll be gone — and be a good deal lighter for the night she's spent here in the bay!'

'There's another boat! A little one, like ours,' cried Catriona softly, her sharp eyes spotting a dark shape drifting like a phantom across the lapping water. 'There're two of them! Can you see them, Morgan? Are they coming from the *Candeloro*?'

'Aye, they are!' Morgan muttered an oath. 'They're not waiting for nightfall!' he breathed, thinking aloud. 'They're using the fog to — '

He suddenly glanced around at Catriona, as though for a few seconds he had forgotten her very presence.

'Lie down flat, miss!' he ordered sharply. 'Don't make a sound. Even a whisper carries like a pistol-crack in fog!'

Catriona caught his urgency, and was alarmed. 'What is — '

Morgan silenced her, his fingertip resting against her lips. 'We must not be seen nor heard, miss!'

Catriona lay still on the rough floor

of the boat, her muscles tense, her heart pounding at the unseen, unknown danger.

Candeloro's boats passed by, so close Catriona could smell the acrid smoke of the sailors' pipe tobacco. Seconds stretched endlessly until at last Morgan touched her shoulder.

'It's safe. But stay quiet!' he warned, his mouth pressed close to her ear. 'The *Candeloro* may put out other boats . . . '

When they reached shore, Morgan raised his face, scanning the rise of dunes and woodland beyond. 'We'll circle through Spinney and around to Pelham,' he decided. 'It's best we not go back along the beach, lest one of them spots us.'

'Why must we hide from them?' Catriona exclaimed, speaking for the first time since she'd sighted the *Candeloro* at anchor. 'Who are they?'

'Smugglers, miss,' he answered shortly.

'You've been watching the *Candeloro*.' Catriona looked up at him curiously. 'You even went out sailing today to be sure the vessel was her. You *knew* she was a smuggler, didn't you?'

'Miss,' began Morgan, when Catriona had fallen into step alongside him and they were starting through thickly wooded Spinney, 'smugglers are a cut-throat band. It'd be safest if you don't let on what you've seen this afternoon. And there's something else — ' He paused awkwardly, not meeting Catriona's questioning eyes. 'It's not my place to beg a favour, miss — and I don't like to do it, either.'

'What is it, Morgan?' she murmured encouragingly.

'I'd be obliged if you didn't tell that I use the boat,' he said at length.

'Who would I tell? My uncle? Or Julian?' she demanded. 'How can you think I'd ever give you away to them? You're the only person at Pelham who's been kind to me, Morgan! You're my friend!' Catriona cried passionately. 'I would never betray you — to anybody!'

'I'm obliged, miss,' he said humbly,

looking down into her earnest eyes. 'And I mean you no disrespect, but I can't be your friend. Nor you mine. It wouldn't be proper, and the Espleys wouldn't allow it.'

'Because you're their hired hand?' she retorted in disgust. 'That's nonsense, Morgan!'

'It's the way of the world, miss,' he replied mildly, guiding her through a copse and out of Spinney.

'It's still nonsense,' Catriona maintained stubbornly, as the chimneys of Pelham became visible through the drifting fog. 'And whatever my uncle and cousin would say — you're *still* my friend!'

* * *

'Judge Loxwood is outside with some soldier boys!' Eliza called next morning, sauntering along the hall from Pelham's great front door just as Julian was coming downstairs. 'He's looking for the Master.'

79

'So are half the creditors in Liverpool!' grinned Julian, rubbing a hand carelessly over the coarse beard shadow upon his cheek. 'However, since the old man is out on another of his trips, the good judge and his military pals will have to scour every grog-shop between here and New Brighton to find him!'

'I did tell Judge Loxwood no-one at Pelham knew nothing about the smuggling,' Eliza sniffed imperiously. 'But he insists on seeing somebody.'

Catriona crouched on the landing, watching through the balustrade as Julian pulled open the door and strode outside. Darting into one of the unused bedrooms, Catriona peered down at the horsemen assembled in the driveway.

There was an elderly gentleman dressed in civilian clothes, whom she assumed to be Judge Loxwood, and the much younger Captain of the Command, who led a party of four soldiers.

Julian and the judge were conversing; Julian shrugging and shaking his head. Judge Loxwood was nodding gravely, and the party turned to leave.

Catriona wandered across to her own room and found Eliza there, putting clean linen onto the bed.

'For all his fancy talk about smashing the smugglers and the wreckers,' Eliza commented sagely, 'the judge'll not catch them, y'know. He never has and he never will!'

'Why not?' queried Catriona.

'Because they're clever — and because local folk cover up for 'em!'

'Isn't that dangerous?'

'Well, of course it's dangerous, miss!' Eliza retorted scornfully. 'Smugglers, or anybody caught helping them, hang for sure. But you see, the smugglers bring goods folk couldn't afford else. And don't run away with the idea it's only poor folk mixed up in it, either! There's half the gentry in the county filling their cellars with smuggled brandy and rum. Not Judge Loxwood, though,' the maid concluded disparagingly. 'A long streak of misery, he is. Just like that old maid daughter of his!'

'What's Maud like?' asked Catriona curiously.

'Dull as dishwater,' Eliza replied acidly. 'Wrong side o' thirty, and all!'

'Julian must love her,' considered Catriona.

'Why? Because he's fixing to marry her?' demanded Eliza sarcastically. 'Julian'll only wed Maud Loxwood for the dowry she brings with her!'

★ ★ ★

'Whoa!'

Morgan slowed the horse on the road from Friars Quay village to Pelham, bringing the waggon to a standstill alongside the hedgerow where Catriona was picking berries.

'Blackberry-and-apple pie for tea, is it, miss?'

'Preserves!' Catriona replied with a smile. 'Hannah said I can put up some jars to take home for Robert, Sophy and Granny. Actually, I've been looking out for you to come,' she added, gazing up at him hopefully. 'Is there — '

'Aye, there is, miss!' laughed Morgan, taking a letter from his pocket and handing it to her.

'At last!' Catriona exclaimed jubilantly; however, her face fell as she recognised the handwriting. 'Oh! It's from *Sophy*! Wasn't there anything else for me?'

'Not today,' Morgan answered sympathetically. 'You were expecting something from your young man?'

Catriona nodded bleakly. 'I haven't heard from Granny for a while, but Robert always writes so regularly — I just can't understand why I haven't had a letter from him for weeks now!'

'Must be hard for you,' Morgan commented, steadying the horse as a hare darted across her path and away down amongst the dunes. 'Being parted from your sweetheart.'

'It is awful, Morgan!' confessed Catriona ardently. 'I never imagined I could miss anybody so badly.'

'Not long to wait now, miss.' Morgan

smiled. 'You'll be off home at the end of next month.'

'It seems an eternity away!' she grimaced, taking up the basket brimming with plump, blue-black berries. 'May I come back with you?'

'Surely!' He sprang down, and helped Catriona up onto the waggon seat.

'Morgan, you can read and write, you know about the sea and ships and horses and gardening and carpentry and a host of other crafts,' began Catriona when they were jogging out towards the shore. 'Why do you remain at Pelham?'

'My schooling was cut short, miss,' Morgan answered after a moment, smiling wryly. 'I stay to complete my education. I borrow books from Pelham's library. They're not missed because neither of the Espleys have set foot in that room since your aunt left!'

'You're teasing me!' reproved Catriona with a frown. 'That can't be the only reason?'

'It's one of them. I *do* intend learning more, and Pelham's the place for me to do that,' Morgan replied seriously. 'I've nothing of my own, miss. Not a farthing. Finding work elsewhere wouldn't be easy for somebody like me.'

'Because of your father, you mean?' she enquired tentatively.

Morgan inclined his head reluctantly. 'There are people who believed in my father's innocence. Your Aunt Amanda did, and Judge Loxwood, too.'

Morgan drove the waggon through Pelham's gates and around the drive into the archway.

'Judge Loxwood presided over Pa's trial. He could've ordered execution instead of a life sentence — '

Redbird's hoofbeats galloped up alongside them, and Julian reined in to a canter as he passed the waggon.

'Had a pleasant afternoon with your playmate, Catriona?' He grinned, dismounting and leaving the mare sweating and blowing as he strode towards the house. 'At least while Morgan's entertaining you, he's earning his keep. Lord knows, he's precious little use at anything else!'

Catriona scrambled from the waggon and raced after Julian, her blood boiling. 'How dare you, Julian!' she exploded indignantly the instant they were behind closed doors.

Julian calmly ignored her outrage, stripping off his coat and shirt and tossing them across a chair-back as he crossed to the sink. 'Be a good girl and fetch me a pitcher of hot water.'

'Heat it yourself! You know where the fire is,' she retorted, incensed at his arrogance. 'You shouldn't be washing in the kitchen anyway — Hannah doesn't like it.'

'Hannah is a servant — just like Morgan Chappel,' remarked Julian, lifting the copper of warmed water to the sink. 'Morgan has obviously impressed you greatly with his rustic skills. However, they wouldn't take him very far if I had a fancy to dismiss him from Pelham. A gaol-bird's son without character references would either starve or submit to the workhouse.' He laughed unpleasantly. 'It might be a diverting entertainment to discover which fate awaits Morgan, might it not, cousin?'

'You are despicable, Julian!' breathed Catriona, her angry eyes aflame. 'Morgan's twice the man you are, or ever could be!'

Julian towelled himself down, his attention riveted upon the hot brilliance her furious loyalty was bringing to Catriona's eye and cheek.

'Well, well. Life is certainly filled with surprise,' he murmured in a slow voice. 'Our country kitten has some sharp claws!'

Even as rage against him burned deep within her, Catriona was keenly aware that Julian was looking at her in a way he never had before.

★ ★ ★

Hannah gave a relieved sigh as she closed the door against the blustery autumnal day.

'Happen we'll get some peace and quiet now Mister Julian's off to stay with the Ashmoores,' she commented, returning to her baking board. 'Mind, I'm not sure I wouldn't rather the Master be ranting and raving, instead of mouldering round miserable as second skimmings the way he is now.'

'He seems to be getting worse,' Catriona said from the chimney-corner, where she was toasting her toes before the fire.

'Don't reckon he'll ever get better, miss,' Hannah considered grimly. 'Doctor's warned him, but he pays no heed. Last night, when Morgan was getting him upstairs, I swear if the Master could've got to his own feet, he'd have flattened the lad good and proper!'

'How long has Morgan been at Pelham, Hannah?'

'Just after Morgan's father was arrested, Mrs Chappel and her daughter took influenza and died,' explained Hannah. 'Morgan was only a lad, and he got sent to the orphanage.

'Your Aunt Amanda took pity on him and rescued him. Brought him to Pelham, she did. Made him part of the family, like one of her own children,' Hannah's mouth tightened into a straight line. 'Even had him taught his lessons alongside Mister Julian — you can picture how *that* went down with a certain party!'

'Is that why Julian hates Morgan so?' Catriona asked quietly. 'Because he was jealous?'

'What young gentleman wouldn't be, miss?' demanded Hannah stiffly. 'A lad like Morgan — whose father done what Arfon Chappel done — brought in and treated like royalty! Wasn't proper, miss. Anyhow, when Amanda left Pelham, things were soon set to rights.'

'You mean Morgan was banished to the stables,' Catriona added coldly. 'Forced to become the Espleys' hired hand!'

Hannah sniffed. 'Morgan's a good

enough lad, I'll not say different, but when all's said and — '

She was interrupted by a hasty rapping at the kitchen door.

'I'll answer it.' Catriona hurried to the door. 'Why, hello, Huddy!'

'How do, miss.' The wee lad from the coaching inn was breathing hard from running. 'Letter for you, miss. I got told to bring it to you quick.'

Catriona was transfixed by the sombre black edging to the letter. Her heart froze. Snatching the letter from Huddy's grimy hands, she frantically tore it open.

'Miss?' Hannah bustled to her side. 'You've gone white as a sheet, lass!'

'Granny.' Catriona was trembling, her legs suddenly unable to support her weight. 'She . . . she's . . . '

'Sit yourself down.' Hannah pushed Catriona into a chair.

'No! No, I can't,' Catriona protested agitatedly, struggling unsteadily to her feet. 'I must go home straight away, Hannah!'

'Nay, nay, miss — just be still and take a breath,' returned Hannah sensibly. 'We don't even know when the next coach is due.'

'I don't care!' Catriona cried desperately. 'I have to get home!'

'Course you do, miss,' Hannah agreed quickly. 'You sit down before you fall down, while I go up and pack your bits. Soon as Morgan's back from driving Mister Julian's luggage to the Ashmoores, he can take you to the coach.'

'You're not going anywhere, Catriona!'

Both women spun around as though thunderstruck. Neither one had noticed Samuel Espley listening from the doorway into the hall.

'Uncle, it's *Granny*!' blurted Catriona brokenly, starting past him towards the stairs. 'I'm going home!'

'I told you!' Samuel Espley grasped her wrist tightly, forcing Catriona back around to face him. 'You are not leaving this house!'

Catriona stared up at him with

sorrow-filled eyes. 'You don't understand, Uncle,' she began patiently. 'I'm taking the next northbound coach.'

'Your grandmother is dead.' Espley's voice was hard, void of emotion. 'I am your legal guardian now. And you *will* remain at Pelham!'

'I won't . . . I *won't* . . . ' Catriona shook her head over and over again, backing away from Samuel Espley, tears of grief and pain spilling uncontrollably from her eyes. 'I'm not a prisoner. You can't keep me here!'

Spinning around, she tore open the kitchen door and fled across the garden.

Catriona ran and ran until her heart was hammering and her lungs felt they must surely burst. Stumbling to her knees, she crumpled to the coarse grass of the dunes and gave vent to her aching loss and utter helplessness.

★   ★   ★

There it was Morgan Chappel found her, as night darkened the shore.

'I've just got back from the Ash-moores. Hannah told me about your granny,' he muttered, kneeling at Catriona's side as she lay face-down, her head buried into her folded arms. 'I'm so very sorry, miss.'

Morgan reached out his hand, gently touching her shoulder. 'Dear Lord, you're half-frozen — '

Pulling off his coarse-woven coat, Morgan lifted Catriona's frail, trembling body and enveloped the thick garment around her.

'I wish there was something I could say to make the hurt less,' he whispered, chafing her icy hands within his own. 'But there isn't, Catriona. There isn't a single thing.'

'Oh, Morgan!' Catriona raised dry, anguished eyes to his earnest face. 'She was all alone. I wasn't there with her!'

Morgan impulsively pulled Catriona's shivering body hard against his chest, wrapping his arms tightly about her as much to warm as to comfort her.

6

'Don't torment yourself, miss,' advised Morgan some weeks later. 'It wasn't your fault you weren't allowed to attend your grandmother's burial,' he went on, splitting another log into kindling. 'She'd understand that.'

'I know,' Catriona responded unhappily. 'It just hurts so much that I wasn't there when she needed me most.'

She was desperate to go home to Strathlachie, but Samuel Espley remained utterly relentless.

'I haven't heard from Robert since his letter of condolence,' Catriona told Morgan later that morning as they shared a luncheon of bread and cheese from his snap tin. 'But will you mail this for me? I've written to Robert, asking him to come and fetch me home.

'Robert is to be my husband

— Uncle Samuel *must* listen to him, mustn't he?' she persisted forlornly. 'Robert is my last hope!'

While Catriona counted the days, willing Robert's response to come speedily, she drew strength from knowing soon she would leave Pelham forever and become Robert's wife. Only the notion of leaving behind her dear friendship with Morgan Chappel caused Catriona regret.

For the first time in months, smugglers had been on Friars Quay beach the previous night. From her window, Catriona had spied them: masked and silent, moving from the water's edge and away amongst the cover of the dunes with their kegs of contraband.

She was sitting at her window now, repairing the seam of her thick plaid skirt, and saw Julian galloping into the yard on Redbird, returning from his stay with the Ashmoores.

'May I come in?' he asked, a quarter-hour or so later, sauntering through the open doorway of her room.

'I've just returned home.'

'I saw you,' she remarked indifferently. 'Did you enjoy your visit?'

'It was first-rate! Stayed weeks longer than planned.' He grinned enthusiastically. 'Ended up in London, and had a good time of it there, too!'

Julian paused, clearing his throat almost apologetically. 'The old man's told me about your grandmother. It's rotten luck.'

'Yes,' replied Catriona shortly.

'If it's any consolation, I think the old soak was wrong to keep you from attending the funeral,' Julian offered seriously. 'Whether he admits it or not, my father is no longer Master of Pelham, Catriona. Had *I* been here, I would have put you aboard the coach to Scotland myself!'

'Would you really?' queried Catriona, her hazel eyes flashing challengingly. 'Then do so *now*, Julian!' she cried. 'Defy your father and make good your fine words. Take me to the coaching inn!'

Julian hesitated, his face dark with annoyance.

'Your silence answers me, Julian!' she railed in disgust. 'I was once told you and your father are two of the same kind. Now you prove it true!'

He leaned back against the mantel and surveyed Catriona with a sardonic grin. 'Anything else, sweet cousin?'

'You're weak, Julian! You're a selfish, mean-spirited bully! Worse yet, you're a liar and a cheat. You're deceiving Maud Loxwood!'

'Careful, Catriona!' warned Julian in a low voice. 'You go too far, girl!'

But Catriona would not be intimidated. 'I've never met Maud Loxwood, but she deserves better than to be betrayed! Morgan says she's a fine woman, and — '

'*Morgan says?*' echoed Julian vehemently, all humour vanished. His young cousin's stinging taunts had found their mark, and his anger was cold and dangerous.

'You regard Morgan Chappel as such a strong, honourable knight, don't you?

I'm certain such a paragon of righteousness has told you all about his past?'

'That his father be imprisoned is no fault nor shame of Morgan's!' she cried loyally.

'My word, I do admire your charity and capacity for forgiveness,' he observed slyly. 'I'm not certain I could be quite so magnanimous if *my* parents had drowned aboard the ship Morgan Chappel's father scuppered!'

Catriona ill-concealed her horror at Julian Espley's shocking revelation.

The moment he quit her room, she sped down to the stables and waited in mounting agitation for Morgan to arrive back from Friars Quay village.

'Why didn't you tell me?'

She waylaid him at the stable doors.

'I *trusted* you, Morgan! I believed you were my friend!' Catriona shook her head despairingly. 'I opened my heart to you, and you deceived me!'

He searched her anguished face in consternation.

'Catriona, it isn't as it appears,' he murmured at last. 'I didn't ever lie to you.'

'Nor did you tell me the truth!' she cut in quietly. 'We've spoken about my parents — about the way they died. Why didn't you *tell* me your father was captain of the *Rhiannon*?'

'In the beginning, I thought you must know,' Morgan answered simply. 'Then, well, how could I just come out and say something like that? And later, when we really became friends — ' His eyes fleetingly met hers. ' — I had started to hope that perhaps it wouldn't matter so much to you, Catriona.'

'Wouldn't matter?' she cried, her voice rising shrilly. 'Your father murdered my parents!'

Morgan's response could not have been more acute had she struck him.

'My father's an innocent man, miss,' he said curtly, fighting to restrain his own turbulent emotions. 'However, supposing he *were* guilty of what you say, would his crime make me guilty, too?

'For all your noble talk of loyalty and friendship, you're no better than the rest of them!' he finished bitterly, his taut resolve ultimately breaking. 'You're looking at me now, Catriona, but all you can see is the hired hand who's a gaol-bird's son!'

Morgan strode away from her in disgust, as an afterthought turning and retrieving a letter from his coat pocket.

'My apologies, miss. I was forgetting. There's a letter for you.'

His attitude was deliberately servile, but his eyes were blazing with contempt, and Catriona was unable to meet their searing gaze as she stepped forward to receive the long-awaited reply from Robert.

Stalking stiff-backed from the stables, Catriona made her way to the snow-dusted beach where she could be certain of privacy.

Sheltering from the biting north-westerly wind, she sat upon the steps of the boathouse and eagerly began reading Robert's letter.

As she took in the words, Catriona's blood turned to ice in her veins.

I have to ask you to release me from my promise to marry you, wrote Robert, formally. *Sophy and I are in love . . .*

Robert, and the girl who was dearer than a sister to Catriona?

It wasn't true! It *couldn't* be. Catriona loved them both so much. They wouldn't hurt her like this.

The writing on the page blurred in front of her, but Catriona couldn't weep. She felt numb. As though she'd never be capable of trusting or feeling love ever again.

She'd believed herself betrayed by Morgan Chappel. But now, Catriona knew the bitterest betrayal of all.

She remained at the boathouse, until the incoming tide brought dark waves crusted with ice up onto the beach and cast them at her feet.

All of Catriona's hopes, her whole life and future, were tumbling down about her. Even Morgan Chappel's stalwart companionship was now lost to her. She knew she must somehow get away from Pelham.

By midnight, Julian was out and Eliza had gone home. Hannah had retired for the night, and by good fortune Uncle Samuel was still in the drawing-room, slumbering off the effects of his latest jaunt into town.

Catriona packed a change of clothes and a few personal belongings into a small bundle. The rest of her possessions must be left behind. In her stockinged feet, she crept down the back stairs, through the deserted kitchen, and, with pounding heart, darted out into the cloud-ridden, moonless night and across the cobbled yard.

Catriona let herself noiselessly into the stables, aware Morgan Chappel was sleeping only a few yards away up in the hayloft. The slightest sound might awaken him and bring him down to investigate. Catriona was so tense she could scarcely breathe, but her determination was steeled.

Resting her bundle into the straw, Catriona padded along the line of stalls, shushing the horses as they stirred and whickered curiously.

'Easy, girl! Easy,' she crooned into the ear of the grey mare, slipping a bridle onto the animal. 'Shhh, it's all right — '

'Catriona!'

A cry of alarm escaped her lips as she felt a hand upon her arm, whirling around to see Morgan, barefoot and wearing only breeches, his blue-black hair tousled from sleep.

'Whatever are you doing?'

'Leaving Pelham,' she returned, every inch of her taut as a coiled spring. 'Robert's marrying Sophy. But I'm going home to Strathlachie anyway. It's where I belong.'

'It's madness, Catriona.' He caught her by the shoulders, bringing her around to face him. 'You can't!'

'Then I'll die trying!' she whispered vehemently. 'You won't stop me, Morgan!'

He held onto her fiercely, staring down into her eyes for a long moment.

'I'll go with you.' Morgan said finally. 'I don't — '

The stable door flung back on its hinges and a flurry of fine rain blew within. Lantern-light flooded over Catriona and Morgan, and Morgan instinctively drew the girl closer to him as Samuel Espley stood framed by the doorway.

Espley's raddled face contorted with rage as he beheld his niece in the naked arms of the hired hand.

'Saw you sneaking out here,' he mumbled thickly, his words sliding drunkenly one into the next. '*Harlot!*'

Espley staggered forwards, violently setting aside the lantern so it threw grotesque images leaping and crouching about the stables' stone walls. The horsewhip in his hands flicked as he reached out for Catriona.

Morgan threw her to the straw as the whip sliced through the air, taking its stinging lash broad across his chest.

'I asked her to meet me, Master!' he shouted, using his body to block Samuel Espley's getting any closer to Catriona. 'Miss wanted to go back up to the house — I wouldn't let her go!'

Catriona heard her own voice crying out unintelligibly. It was her fault! Not Morgan's. None of it was his fault! Why didn't her uncle hear her? Why didn't he stop?

Catriona was down on the ground, her knees drawn tight to her body, staring with horrified eyes as again and again, Samuel Espley raised the whip, and again and again, Morgan Chappel submitted to the beating.

Morgan was young and strong. Why did he not defend himself?

Catriona was powerless to do anything but watch in mute terror as Samuel Espley exorcised the frenzied violence of his drunken wrath.

Breathing heavily, Espley's head finally dropped onto his chest. His shoulders sagged. Turning clumsily, he staggered across the stable, leaning heavily onto his cane. Staring blankly straight ahead, he half-stumbled out into the drizzle and crossed the yard to the house.

Catriona scrambled to Morgan's side. His back and shoulders were laced with cruel, thin cuts and blistered with angry red weals. He lay sprawled in the straw, horribly still.

'He's not dead, miss.' Eliza sauntered through the open, swinging doors. 'Just passed out.'

Catriona spun around, too relieved at the matter-of-fact reassurance to wonder why the maid was at Pelham so early.

'Help me, Eliza,' she said.

Morgan groaned, shifting slightly. His eyes still closed.

Catriona's attention snapped back to him, but Eliza was already bustling by her.

'I'll tend to him, miss,' the maid said briskly. 'You go back up to the house.'

'No!' Catriona's refusal was adamant. 'Morgan was beaten because of me.'

'I'm sure he was, miss,' Eliza remarked acidly. 'But you can't do no good for him now. The master'll likely already be sleeping it off, and won't remember a thing when he does wake up. But if by chance he *should* take it into his head to get up and wander out again, and he catches *you* still in here . . . '

The maid sucked in her breath meaningfully. 'There'd be no stopping him, miss!'

Morgan was starting to come round, and Eliza bent to him, so he was able to lean against her.

'Get yourself into the house, miss.' repeated the maid, not sparing Catriona another glance. 'And stay there!'

Catriona was loath to abandon Morgan. However, there was sense in Eliza's warning about Samuel Espley. Sick with guilt and remorse, Catriona reluctantly acquiesced.

Pausing at the stable doorway, she lingered but a moment to watch as, with Morgan's arm draped over her shoulders, Eliza wrapped her own arms about him and helped him to his feet. Catriona was ashamed of the jealousy she felt.

If Samuel Espley did retain any recollection of his actions that damp, drizzly night, he made no reference to it. Sober and groomed, he emerged from Pelham late the following morning and bid Catriona a gracious goodbye, was tolerably civil to Morgan as he mounted his horse, and, with an amiable nod at Julian, cantered through the archway and away towards town.

'That's the last we'll see of the old man until he's full and his pockets are empty,' Julian remarked, pausing alongside Catriona on the stone steps.

'I returned too late for last night's excitement,' he went on wryly. 'However, I gather Morgan Chappel took quite a thrashing for your sake! Hmm, you might well be worth it at that, cousin!'

Laughing heartily, Julian disappeared indoors, and Catriona went hesitantly to the vegetable garden. Morgan was working, as on any other day, and the uncharacteristic tension of his muscles and movement were the only indications of the terrible beating he'd suffered on her behalf.

'Are you alright?' she asked him softly.

'I am,' he replied politely. 'Thank you, miss.'

'Why did you let Uncle Samuel go on believing you and I were . . . ' Catriona faltered uncomfortably. 'I would've owned up to the truth, Morgan! Why did you prevent my doing so?'

'I know Samuel Espley better than you do, miss. I know what he's capable of,' replied Morgan evenly, never pausing in his work as he spoke. 'The mood Master was in — if he'd learned you were running away, there's no guessing what he would've done! The Master doesn't remember last night, and you and I are the only others who know what happened,' he concluded firmly. 'It's gone and done with, miss.

No cause to say more about it.'

Catriona felt he was dismissing her, exactly as Eliza had done in the stable; however, she hovered uncertainly. 'Morgan. Can we go back to the way we were before we quarrelled? Be friends again?'

'That's for you to decide, miss,' he answered unemotionally.

'Perhaps we can never put things back exactly,' she conceded unwillingly. 'But we can begin again, can't we? I don't want to lose your friendship, Morgan!'

He stopped working, and really looked at her. Catriona felt his level gaze upon her, aware that colour was rising to her cheeks as Morgan's clear blue eyes penetrated to her very soul.

'Nor I yours,' he responded at length.

She smiled thankfully up at him, experiencing a kind of shyness she'd never before known with Morgan.

★　★　★

With the coming of spring, Catriona began reviving Amanda Espley's walled flower garden, and spent many contented hours planting and nurturing lavender, primroses and bell flowers.

Grandmother McPherson's cottage had been duly cleared, and occupied by new tenants. The village choirmaster, Oliver Stuart, had forwarded a few of Essie McPherson's personal effects to Catriona at Pelham.

Opening the package, and seeing again the few possessions Granny had especially cherished, evoked poignant memories for Catriona. She stood the posy bowl on her mantel, hung the watercolour miniature her mother had painted of Strathlachie's glen upon the wall of her room, and began setting the small collection of well-read books onto the shelf.

Catriona thoughtfully considered the volume of Burns, and hurried down to the stables.

'It's beautiful, Catriona!' Morgan exclaimed when she presented him with the book of verse. 'However, I can't possibly accept it!'

'Please do, Morgan,' she insisted quietly.

'It belonged to your grandmother,' he protested gently. 'It means so much to you!'

'It does, and I really want you to have it,' Catriona said; adding, with a mischievous little smile, 'If it will make you feel easier about accepting, in return for the book, you must promise to read to me the very next time we're out in the boat!'

'Done!' Morgan laughed. 'Although you do realise I don't have your fine Scottish accent to do Burns justice!'

'You recite splendidly!' Catriona returned, who thoroughly enjoyed the all-too-rare occasions when they went sailing and would read poetry together, or simply talk about anything and everything.

Still smiling as she left the stables, Catriona almost collided with Julian galloping into the cobbled yard.

'Ah! Do I detect a certain becoming sparkle in your eye? A revealing lightness to your step, Catriona?' he chided drily. 'Your cheek tellingly warm with regard for our humble hired hand?'

Julian swung down from the saddle, sidling alongside her.

'Tell me just one thing,' he murmured confidentially. 'Do you actually *like* Morgan's hayloft?'

Catriona had never seen, nor set foot in, Morgan's room, although she refrained from adding to her cousin's spurious amusement by protesting as much. Julian's merciless taunting about her friendship with Morgan no longer stung nor embarrassed Catriona as it once had done. However, she could not truthfully deny the tender feelings the softness of Morgan's voice, the fleeting touch of his hand against her own, and the very nearness of him whenever they were alone together, provoked within her.

Falling in love with Morgan Chappel

would be so dangerously easy, Catriona realised, wandering into her garden to gather daffodils.

She must not allow it to happen.

Loving him would be foolish and hopeless. It could end only in her being hurt all over again.

And more than anything in the world, Catriona feared the pain of losing love. That awful, aching agony of having her heart broken and suddenly being completely alone.

Catriona was still in her garden when she heard a tremendous commotion from the house, and Eliza came racing through the tall gateway towards her.

'Come quick, miss! It's the Master!'

The two young women ran from the walled garden and into Pelham.

'A couple of carters fetched him home, miss!' Eliza was explaining breathlessly. 'Said they found him by the side of the road. They reckoned he'd been thrown from his horse!'

'So drunk he fell off, more like!' Julian's scathing remark came as he followed the women into the drawing-room.

However, Catriona heard her cousin's sharp intake of breath when he set eyes upon his father, looking whiter than death and lying motionless on the couch with Hannah agitatedly attending to him.

'Eliza,' said Catriona, turning to the maid, 'ask Morgan to go and fetch Doctor Liddle at once.'

She moved toward her cousin, saying, 'Julian, it's cold in here. Get a fire started while Hannah and I try to make your father more comfortable.'

'What?' He stared at her, before nodding absently. 'Er . . . yes . . . yes, of course.'

When Archibald Liddle arrived, Catriona waited with Julian outside the drawing-room while the physician made his examination.

Both Catriona and Julian started to their feet as the drawing-room door opened and Doctor Liddle came soberly out into the hall.

'I've warned Samuel again and again that liquor would be the death of him,' the physician said bluntly. 'Therefore, I sincerely trust he regards this unfortunate episode as a salutary lesson to mend his ways.'

'He'll be all right, then?' Julian expelled a heavy breath.

'This time, yes. But he's a sick man, Julian. Your father was likely lying out on that road twelve or more hours. He's feverish, weak as a babe, and in need of constant nursing until I say otherwise.'

'Hannah and I will care for him, Doctor Liddle,' said Catriona softly.

The physician gave a long-suffering nod and took his hat from the stand. 'Heaven help you both! When your uncle awakens, you may inform him that if those carters hadn't discovered him when they did, he wouldn't have needed a doctor today but the coffin-maker!'

Hannah and Catriona shared the tasks of nursing Samuel Espley. Improvement in his condition was slow, and Samuel was a difficult and ungrateful patient. He demanded brandy and tobacco, and became foul-tempered and abusive when these were denied him.

One sticky, stifling day, when Samuel was being particularly truculent and Hannah was by turns bullying and cajoling to placate him while Catriona coped in the kitchen, Julian breezed through with the nonchalant swagger of one who hasn't a care in the world. Debonairly outfitted and freshly barbered, he held out a watermarked silk neckerchief to Catriona.

'Can't get the blasted thing right. Tie it for me, won't you?'

'I'm busy, and my hands are floury,' she remarked shortly, turning back to her bread-making. Julian had not lifted a finger to help during his father's illness, and the brief moment of vulnerability he'd displayed had swiftly vanished into his customary arrogance.

'Eliza!' Julian beckoned the maid, offering the neckerchief. 'A job for you!'

'There!' Eliza tied the knot with satisfaction, patting it lightly into place against Julian's throat. 'Very handsome, sir!'

'Many thanks, Eliza. It is indeed refreshing to see a face that is not as sour as cheap wine.' He paused, directing a scornful glance in Catriona's direction. 'What ails you, cousin?'

'You might make yourself useful here at Pelham, Julian! Goodness knows, with your father the way he is, there's plenty to be done,' Catriona returned irritably. 'Instead, you amuse yourself gadding around the county!'

'Gadding?' mocked Julian. 'I have important affairs requiring my constant attention!'

'I can guess where,' retorted Catriona darkly. '*And* with whom!'

'Then you'd be mistaken, my dear cousin!' he replied smoothly. 'As well as calling at the offices of Espley Shipping in Liverpool today, I also have a pressing engagement with Maud's father. Not at Larks Grange and of a personal nature, I hasten to add, but at Judge Loxwood's chambers. I fancy he seeks my advice upon capturing the smugglers.'

'If that is truly the purpose of your business, then I sincerely hope you are able to assist the judge,' replied Catriona soberly. 'Those fiends are not the benign benefactors they're oft made out to be!'

That night, it took almost three hours for Catriona and Hannah to persuade Samuel Espley to drink his medicine and settle down. When at last he slept, Hannah rolled her eyes to the heavens.

'Praise be!' she muttered. 'You go up to bed, miss. I'll sit with the Master.'

'Are you sure?' Catriona queried, glancing doubtfully at her uncle. 'What if he awakens?'

'I'll likely hit him over the head with summat heavy!'

'That sounds a sterling idea.' Catriona smiled. 'Good-night, Hannah. Call me if need be.'

The night was hot and airless.

Catriona wearily wandered to the kitchen in search of a cooling drink, and was startled when she came upon Julian seated there in the darkness.

'My goodness!' She gasped. 'I didn't know you were back!'

'Been back for hours,' he commented morosely. 'I've been sitting here in the dark.'

'But not alone,' Catriona remarked scathingly, eyeing the decanter of brandy at his elbow.

'Comfort, Catriona,' he answered with a self-pitying sigh. 'For my future is in ruins. My plan to marry Maud Loxwood, resurrect Pelham and save the Espley Shipping Line . . . all ruined!'

In spite of her disapproval, Catriona was curious.

'Whatever did Judge Loxwood say to you?'

'Well, dear cousin, rumours have reached the judge's honourable ears of my liaison with a married woman.'

'You astound me, Julian!' Catriona

stared at him in disbelief. 'Your own actions brought you to this shameful situation, yet you haven't a shred of remorse or regret for the unhappiness you've caused Maud!'

'I shouldn't have expected sympathy from you, Catriona,' said Julian, his gaze suddenly focusing astutely upon her.

'The worst thing one person can do to another,' she began earnestly, 'is betray their trust!'

'Catriona . . . You've a tender heart,' he said in a low voice, catching hold of both her hands and drawing her closer. 'Don't waste it upon that hired hand — show me a little of your tenderness!'

She impatiently jerked free and started for the door; but, reaching for her waist, Julian caught Catriona off-balance and deftly brought her down across his lap.

'Let me go!' she cried indignantly and, struggling against his embrace, angrily drew back her hand to strike him.

At once, Julian's strong fingers encircled her wrist; arching Catriona back against his free arm, his demanding lips sought a response from hers.

She was breathing fast when Julian finally released her from his kiss.

Scrambling from his lap, Catriona's soft lips felt bruised from the hard pressure of Julian's mouth against her own, and her pulse and senses were racing. 'You're drunk!' she spat in disgust.

'I've been drinking, but not so much I don't know what I'm doing.'

'Then you might do something useful, and sit with your father tonight!' retorted Catriona, smoothing down her rumpled dress and trying to regain her dignity. 'Hannah would certainly welcome the respite.'

Quitting the kitchen, she went up to the sanctuary of her own room. From caution, Catriona did not light her candle, for yet again the silhouettes of men filing stealthily along the shore were distinct against the silvery tide, once more successfully outwitting the soldiers and evading capture.

When she lay on her bed, she heard Julian going outdoors for his horse. He had not taken her suggestion to sit with Uncle Samuel, but then not for a moment had Catriona expected he would.

7

That year there was an Indian summer, with the hot, dry weather lasting far into September.

Catriona was dressed in her coolest cotton. She reached into her drawer for her mother's amethyst brooch — but it wasn't where she was certain she had left it!

'Eliza!' Catriona went to her door, calling the maid as she sauntered along the landing with Julian's shirt draped over her bare arm. 'Have you seen my brooch?'

'I'm sure I haven't, miss!' Eliza retorted, her eyes darting to Julian emerging from his room. 'Why?'

'I didn't intend on snapping at you, Eliza,' Catriona went on apologetically. 'I'm worried because it's mislaid. It belonged to my mother, and was the last thing Granny gave me before I left home.'

'I'll keep my eyes open for it then, miss,' answered Eliza curtly, squeezing by Julian to get on with her duties.

Catriona thoroughly searched her room, then took out each of her garments and shook it gently, lest the cherished brooch be caught amongst the folds. Long hours of meticulous searching failed to reveal the whereabouts of her beloved brooch, however, and Catriona had no choice but to hope it would somehow eventually be found.

She awoke early next morning and, in spite of having lost her brooch, was looking forward to the day ahead with eager anticipation. Morgan had agreed to take her on a picnic at Beacon Point. Catriona sang softly as she dressed in a rather becoming cream muslin, but was more than a little sad at not being able to pin the amethyst brooch upon the dress's neat scalloped collar.

Tripping lightly into the kitchen, she unexpectedly came upon Eliza pirouetting on a chair.

'Ever so pretty, isn't it?' the maid was saying, swirling a brightly-coloured gypsy shawl with shimmering gold tassels about her shoulders. 'When he gave it to me, I could've — oh, sorry, miss! Didn't hear you coming in.'

Eliza jumped down from the chair, folding the shawl decoratively about her arms.

'I was showing Hannah my new shawl, miss,' she went on, with a pert grin. 'Nice, isn't it?'

'Very,' replied Catriona with a stiff smile, for the loss of her amethyst brooch and Eliza's sudden possession of a new shawl flashed together into her mind.

She was at once ashamed of the ugly suspicion. It was wrong and unfair to doubt Eliza's honesty ... but how could the maid afford even such gaudy finery?

'Present from an admirer, it was,' Eliza volunteered smugly, as though reading Catriona's thoughts.

Catriona nodded, tying the ribbons

126

of her straw sun-bonnet, uncertain whether to believe Eliza's plausible explanation.

She was still deliberating a little later when Morgan came into the kitchen to fetch the luncheon basket, and they set off together in the waggon for Beacon Point.

★　★　★

It was later that evening that Catriona was quietly playing the harpsichord, her thoughts still distracted.

Julian hadn't yet returned from a trip to Liverpool; so, with Uncle Samuel out on an ill-advised jaunt, Eliza gone home, and Hannah visiting her brother over at Sandford, Catriona was on her own in the rambling house.

All in all, Catriona was considerably relieved when she heard Julian's horse.

He came into the room sombre-faced, and said nothing. He simply withdrew a handkerchief from his waistcoat pocket, opened the folds, and laid it down upon the keys of the harpsichord.

'My amethyst brooch!' Catriona exclaimed in delight. 'Oh, Julian! Thank you! Wherever did you find it?'

His reply was brusque. 'For sale. In the window of a Liverpool pawnbroker.'

Catriona was shocked. 'Then Eliza did — '

'Not Eliza,' cut in Julian sharply. 'The pawnbroker bought the brooch yesterday, from a man. A man answering to Morgan Chappel's description.'

Catriona's eyes were wide and horrified. She shook her head vehemently.

'You're not telling me the truth. Morgan would never — '

'Catriona, face the facts!' Julian demanded in exasperation. 'You've been lonely and unhappy, and you've seen only what you wished to see in Morgan. What do you actually *know* about him?'

'Everything!' Catriona declared passionately. 'Morgan is my friend.'

'He's used you. He *is* using you!' retorted Julian harshly. 'Morgan stole your brooch, and sold it while he was in Liverpool to buy a fancy frippery for his girl!'

'Eliza's *not* his girl!' cried Catriona in consternation. 'She's not! Oh, once I thought she was, too — but I was wrong! Morgan doesn't even like Eliza very much . . . '

Julian extended his hand challengingly toward Catriona.

'Come with me now! Let us together confront him. *Then* you shall discover for yourself whether it is I, or Morgan Chappel, who is playing you false!'

'I will speak to Morgan in the morning,' she decided, not quite able to still the tremor in her voice. 'And prove your vile accusations wrong!'

With that, Catriona fled to her room, throwing herself fully-dressed onto the bed in a quandary of confusion and despair.

The air was unbearably hot and

oppressive, the rumble of the approaching thunder fusing with insistent pounding of the incoming high tide, drumming through Catriona's troubled mind until she felt as though she would soon lose her reason.

'Catriona! *Catriona!*'

A hand upon her shoulder impatiently shook her awake. She opened swollen eyes, stirring with difficulty from a restless slumber that had been unnaturally deep and heavy.

'Julian?' she mumbled. 'What's — '

'For pity's sake, girl. *Come!*' He half-dragged her from the bed, his face and countenance taut with urgency. 'Come to the beach — hurry!'

Redbird was waiting, saddled and sweating from already having been ridden too hard. Julian mounted swiftly, hauling the still-dazed Catriona up across the saddle in front of him. Kicking the mare into a fast gallop, Julian rode north in the direction of Beacon Point.

The tide was at high water when

130

Julian finally halted Redbird in the dark concealment of a stand of gorse bushes surrounding the small cottage which had been Morgan Chappel's childhood home. Swinging from the saddle, Julian unceremoniously pulled Catriona down beside him.

'The smugglers are at work tonight,' he began shortly. 'I realised you would not believe me unless you saw with your own eyes that — '

Catriona wasn't listening.

Gorse Cottage offered a sweeping vista of sea and shore, and Catriona's attention was fastened upon a torch flaring brightly from a short distance along the coast where there should not have been light, while the higher ground of Beacon Point was a well of blackness.

Even in that split-second, Catriona glimpsed the band of shadowy figures waiting far below on the Marram Shore. Saw the masts of the *Isabella*, her sails unfurled and full; the vessel pitching and tossing like a toy ship upon the swollen, churning, black waters as the storm unleashed its fury, spilling a barrage of cold rain like musket fire.

'They're going to wreck her, Julian!' yelled Catriona above the roar and wail of the breaking storm. 'We have to light the beacon on the Point!'

'It's too late. Too late!' he shouted, gripping her arms and holding Catriona back from the smugglers' sight. 'The ship's lost, Catriona. No beacon on earth can save her now!'

The mortal screams of the ship's doomed crew, the wrenching and splintering of mast and timbers, carried sickeningly through the wrath of the storm. Catriona watched in horror as the mighty vessel heaved and foundered amongst the spume-flecked waves, fighting for her life as she crashed again and again against the ruthless comb of rocks.

Suddenly, Julian took Catriona forcibly by the waist, throwing her to the sodden ground and crouching down at her side.

'Catriona. Over there — ' he breathed, pointing toward where the false light had burned. '*Look!*'

The torch was but a spitting ember now, and the solitary man carrying it was striding along the darkness of the shore while the smugglers put out into the shallows, hungry for the *Isabella*'s ample riches.

The man stood straight and still for a moment, before violently thrusting the torch deep into the wet sand to finally extinguish its treachcrous light.

But in the dying flame of that wrecker's torch, Catriona clearly saw the young man's face.

8

' . . . I rode out of the dunes, and saw
smugglers were gathering on the beach,'
Julian told Catriona when they were
safely back at Pelham. 'Morgan Chappel was amongst them.'

He was agitatedly prowling the
dimly-lit kitchen, swilling brandy from
one of Hannah's tin mugs, rainwater
still glistening upon his hair and
clothes.

'I fetched you from your bed to prove
to you that Morgan is *not* the man you
believe him to be. If only I'd had an
inkling of what that fiend was truly
about, I would have raised Loxwood
and the military. It was not mere
smuggling tonight, but *wrecking* — and
I could have stopped him, Catriona!'

'Those poor, poor sailors,' Catriona
whispered brokenly, her face buried in
her hands as she sat hunched into the

chimney corner.

Her head jerked up as she heard the bang of the stable door. Morgan had returned!

'So, he's come back to lie low and play the innocent, has he?' Julian remarked bitterly. 'And not more than a pace or two ahead of the soldiers, I'll wager. Hark at their pistol fire!'

Catriona did not dare to even speak Morgan's name, for Julian's smouldering fury against him — and against the terrible events they had both witnessed that night — was close to erupting. Catriona feared for what her volatile cousin might do if antagonised.

Despite having seen Morgan down there on the beach, despite the most damning evidence of his wrongdoing being before her own eyes, Catriona still could not believe Morgan capable of such wickedness. She clung desperately to the hope that there was an explanation. That somehow Morgan was blameless, and not responsible for the deaths of all those aboard the *Isabella*.

'Well, at long last, a hasty awakening is in store for our honourable Mister Chappel,' commented Julian grimly. 'For when Judge Loxwood and the military come asking their usual questions, they shall have him!'

'No!' Catriona's retort was an anguished yelp. 'We must at least hear what Morgan has to say. We cannot assume he's guilty and give him up to the soldiers — '

'Catriona.' Julian shook his head contemptuously. 'How in God's name can you still protect him after all you've seen this night?'

'I *trust* Morgan!' she cried despairingly, tearing the admission from deep within her heart. 'I love him, Julian!'

He glared at her, and the atmosphere was charged with unbearable tension as Catriona waited to know what her cousin intended to do.

The silence was split by voices. The clatter of iron-shod hoofs on the cobbles outside.

'They're here!'

'Julian — ' She ran to him, grasping his arm fiercely. 'Please don't tell them about Morgan yet! Let me talk to him first! I'm certain there's — '

Without a word, Julian strode into the yard to greet Judge Loxwood and the Captain of the Command. The red and white of the soldiers' uniforms showed stark against the soft purple dawn, but the men looked defeated and worn, their sweat-streaked horses tired and muddied.

Catriona crept out to Julian's side, her beseeching eyes never leaving his gravely determined face. She was not able to take in Judge Loxwood's crisp enquiries, listening with increasing relief only to Julian's noncommittal answers.

'Thank you, Julian,' she murmured humbly, when the military were turning to leave empty-handed. 'Thank you for not giving him up.'

'I did it only for you, Catriona. Shielding a murderer does not make me proud of myself!' Julian returned savagely. 'You have one hour with your lover . . . then I ride to Larks Grange with the truth of it!'

Catriona made to speed for the stables, but then froze where she stood, shrinking deep into the shadows of the archway.

The stable door was edging open, and Eliza cautiously peeped out, evidently wishing to ensure nobody was around.

She emerged, her pale hair mussed, her clothing in disarray. Sauntering towards the house, she was hurriedly fastening her bodice, straightening her skirts, arranging the brightly-coloured gypsy shawl more neatly about her shoulders.

Catriona's cry of despair was silent.

Past images flooded into her over-wrought mind . . . Eliza and Morgan laughing together . . . The two of them climbing up to the hayloft the night Morgan was whipped . . . The lost brooch . . . Eliza showing off her new

138

gypsy shawl . . . Morgan down on the stormy Marram Shore, the wrecker's light in his hands . . .

Suddenly, Catriona's passionate loyalty snapped. The bitter pain of betrayal engulfed her, bringing in its wake a surge of hot, vengeful fury.

Spinning from the archway, Catriona ran through the blackthorns and down the curving drive, her heart hammering.

'Sir!' she shouted, halting the soldiers as they were passing from Pelham's tall iron gates. 'Judge Loxwood — *wait!*'

★　★　★

In the nights following Morgan Chappel's arrest, Catriona could not close her eyes without again seeing his face — upturned to the window from which Catriona had been watching, his eyes meeting hers even as the soldiers dragged him from the stable to lead him bound and captive on the long march to Liverpool and the Castle Hill gaol.

She felt no remorse. Catriona's heart had hardened against Morgan. Notions of he and Eliza together still tormented her relentlessly.

Although neither Catriona nor Morgan had ever declared their love for each other, it had been implicit in their every look, every word, in the very closeness they'd shared. Yet all the while, Morgan Chappel had been deceiving her. All the time, he'd been furtively meeting Eliza. Secretly loving *her*!

Almost a week went by after Morgan's arrest before Catriona finally came to realise she would never know a second's peace of mind until she confronted Morgan with the seething anger and pain his betrayal had brought her.

When Julian was preparing to leave for the Espley Shipping Company offices, Catriona decided to accompany him into Liverpool. Dressing in her smart grey linen suit, she went downstairs and found Julian in the kitchen, where Eliza was making much of brushing his travelling coat.

The young maid had shown no emotion whatsoever at Morgan's arrest, and Catriona had deliberately taken to avoiding the girl. It was almost unbearable for her to set eyes upon Eliza, knowing she was a partner to Morgan's unfaithfulness.

' — I deserve it!' Eliza was pouting crossly, her pale cheeks flushed by work and annoyance. 'You *promised* I'd be housekeeper at Pelham!'

'So you shall. One day,' replied Julian carelessly, standing while she helped him on with his coat. 'Have you brought down my hat — Catriona!'

He caught sight of her from the corner of his eye.

'Don't stand there hovering, cousin. My word, you're looking very attractive today!'

'May I drive into Liverpool with you, Julian?' she asked clearly, not glancing in Eliza's direction. 'I wish to go to Castle Hill and see Morgan Chappel.'

'I shall be delighted to drive you, cousin!' Julian declared, bowing with a flourish and offering her his arm. 'Though why you want to visit a cold-blooded murderer, I cannot imagine.'

When they arrived in Liverpool, their carriage turned into a wide, steep street.

'Castle Hill is about a mile ahead,' Julian told her. 'A gaol is hardly the place for a lady. Perhaps I ought to accompany you inside?'

'I intend on seeing Morgan Chappel alone,' Catriona replied firmly.

'As you wish.' Julian shrugged. 'However, we may have need of subterfuge to gain your entry.'

Catriona looked disconcerted. 'Surely if I obtain permission from the commander of the garrison — '

'Ah, there's a much easier way to do almost anything — if you use the correct influence!' Julian grinned wryly, driving up before the iron-studded gates of the formidable garrison. 'Every man has his price . . . '

Within minutes, Julian emerged from the watch tower.

'It's arranged, cousin! You may see the condemned man,' he remarked blithely. 'I shall be spending the entire day at the shipping office. Since we no longer have a hired hand, can you drive yourself home to Pelham?'

'Of course,' she answered shortly. 'Morgan taught me.'

'I'm sure he taught you well.' Julian laughed softly, extending his arms to help Catriona down from the carriage. 'And much more besides!'

'You really are loathsome!' returned Catriona with disgust.

'Perhaps, but I now realise I owe Morgan Chappel my deepest gratitude,' began Julian slyly, lifting Catriona to the ground, his hands staying about her slender waist as he considered her appraisingly. 'Nurtured by his bucolic attentions, you have blossomed into quite a beauty, Catriona!'

Pulling free contemptuously, Catriona

walked purposefully towards the massive iron-bound gates of Castle Hill.

She was led across a courtyard where a squad of troops was being drilled, and from there into the gaol itself. Catriona shuddered. Her palms were cold and clammy, and she was finding breathing difficult in the close, fetid air. There were whispering voices, cries, groans and shouts from countless prisoners held within the thick stone walls, but Catriona could think only of one man. And it was she who had condemned him to this hell.

Presently, the turnkey unlocked a door and swung it open, jamming a lit torch into a bracket just within the cell.

'There you go, miss. Now you can see what you're about.' He stood aside for Catriona to enter. 'This lot haven't the strength to give you any trouble, but I'll be outside if you should need me.'

Catriona nearly cried out in panic when the turnkey slammed the door and she heard the lock snap home, imprisoning her in the confines of the low, dank cell. There was no air, no light other than the guttering torch, and it was several moments before she was able to see. Her eyes scanned the filthy, emaciated faces of a score of men shackled hand and foot, crammed together in the small square cell. Too weak even to sit, the prisoners lay in vile straw, staring at her with vacant eyes.

'Morgan!' His name escaped Catriona's lips like a cry of pain.

She ran down the steep steps and straight to his side, her arms embracing him. Fettered and weakened as he was, Morgan found strength enough to roughly push Catriona away.

His penetrating blue eyes were brilliant and blazing with anger as he glared up at her.

'Why have you come, Catriona?' he demanded harshly. 'Do you gloat to see me so humiliated?'

'Morgan . . . I'm so — so — ' stumbled Catriona wretchedly, unable to meet his searing gaze. Unable, even, to *look* at him.

Morgan's skin was streaked with dirt, pocked with open sores. His thick black hair was filthy and matted. Half-naked, the proud man Catriona had unwillingly fallen in love with was now utterly degraded, stripped of every shred of dignity.

'Go away, Catriona,' Morgan said bitterly. 'For God's sake — go!'

Catriona could not stem the tears flooding her eyes. Turning blindly, she almost fell up the stone steps, rapping at the door for the turnkey to open up and release her.

She was beyond the cell, starting along the passageway, when Morgan's yell of anguish railed after her.

'*Catriona — why did you betray me?*'

★   ★   ★

She drove recklessly down the hill and along the waterfront to the offices of the Espley Shipping Line. Darting past the clerk, Catriona burst into Julian's chambers.

'Julian — I've done a most terrible wrong to Morgan!' she cried passionately, her face and neck flushed and perspiring. 'He isn't a wrecker! He isn't, oh, he *isn't*! Don't ask me to explain or prove it, I can't. But I have faith in Morgan Chappel! I trust him, Julian. In my heart, I *know* he couldn't be guilty!'

'A pretty speech indeed, cousin,' remarked Julian from his desk. 'However, it's for a jury to decide now.'

'No!' Catriona shook her head vehemently. 'I gave Morgan up to Judge Loxwood, not because of what we saw on the Marram Shore that night, but because *I* saw Eliza stealing away from Morgan's loft in the stables! And I realised everything you'd told me about the pair of them being lovers was true after all.'

Julian surveyed her curiously. 'You no longer believe that to be so?'

'I no longer *care*!' Catriona cried in

despair. 'Don't you understand? All I care about is having Morgan released from this injustice. I need your help, Julian! What can I do? I must set this to rights, I must! Should I go to Judge Loxwood? Or the Captain of the Command?'

'Won't do an iota of good,' Julian said complacently, pouring a glass of dry Spanish wine. 'Morgan Chappel has to stand trial, and there's an end to it.'

'No, no.' She shook her head, distraught. 'It's my fault Morgan is in prison. I have to get him out — Julian, you have influence. Power. You know the right people. Couldn't you plead for Morgan? Have the charges against him dropped?'

'Not possible. However . . . ' His narrowed eyes were never for a moment leaving Catriona's flushed face as she waited in a passion of anticipation for his response. 'Perhaps I could grease a few palms and have him, shall we say, set free.'

'Do it!' she cried ardently. 'Do it now. Straight away!'

'If I were to do this for you, Catriona, I'd be taking a colossal risk. Suppose my part in the plot were discovered? I'd likely be facing the hangman myself! Why should I put my own life in jeopardy, cousin?' Julian rose, advancing towards Catriona slowly and deliberately. 'What would I gain from this pact?' He smiled wryly at her. 'What will you do to make the danger worth my while?'

'Anything, Julian,' Catriona answered without hesitation. 'I'll do anything!'

'Anything?' Julian repeated, as though savouring the taste of the word upon his tongue. 'That's an enticing offer, cousin. We shall talk of it later.'

9

Catriona was relieved to leave Julian and the teeming port of Liverpool far behind as she drove home to the fresh fields and open sands of Friars Quay.

It was late afternoon when she entered Pelham's kitchen, having decided to tell Eliza of her visit to Castle Hill. She felt it wisest not to say too much, but for Morgan's sake, Catriona could at least ease the maid's mind and give the girl a little hope.

'Where is Eliza?'

'Gone, miss,' Hannah returned grimly.

'Gone home already?' enquired Catriona in surprise. The maid seldom left Pelham before eight o'clock in the evening. 'Or do you mean she's gone on an errand?'

'I mean she's gone for good, miss,' Hannah replied, banging the copper onto the hob. 'Master sent her packing soon as he got back from being out.'

'Why has she been dismissed, Hannah?'

'I wasn't told, and I didn't ask.' The housekeeper pursed her lips.

'Is my uncle in the drawing-room?'

'Master went out again, miss,' said Hannah. 'But I wouldn't worry myself about Eliza, if I was you. She'll land on her feet, all right. Her sort always do!'

Catriona had several hours to compose her thoughts before Julian arrived at Pelham, and presently they went in to dinner together.

During the meal, Catriona was only too well aware Julian was watching her; toying with her; keeping her waiting to learn what conditions she must fulfil to honour her side of their pact.

At length, Julian poured his brandy, lit a cigar, and sat back from the table, gazing across the crisp white linen at her with undisguised pleasure.

'To business, cousin,' he began,

drawing on the cigar. 'Morgan Chappel will duly go free.'

'When?' breathed Catriona, her intense relief and joy obvious for anyone to see.

'The twenty-fourth.'

'That's *weeks* away!' she protested in alarm.

'It is,' Julian agreed indifferently. 'However, you don't imagine such convoluted schemes can be arranged in haste, do you?'

'I suppose not,' conceded Catriona in disappointment, her eyes earnestly searching his face. 'But it is definite, Julian? Morgan *will* be set free?'

'He'll go free.' Julian nodded, reaching for the brandy decanter. 'Now for our pact, cousin. My conditions are threefold.

'When Morgan Chappel is out of gaol, you will neither see him nor seek to contact him. Morgan is never to return to Pelham, or to Friars Quay. And finally, Catriona — ' Julian paused, clearly relishing the absolute power he held over her. ' — I want you for my wife!'

Catriona was aghast. 'You wish me to marry you?'

Julian threw back his head and laughed at her. 'Cousin, I do believe you are more shocked at my honourable proposal than you would have been by a *dishonourable* one!'

Catriona shook her head in disbelief, her thoughts spinning. 'I don't understand,' she commented flatly.

'You regard me a cold-blooded devil, don't you?' Julian enquired wryly. 'I am capable of emotion, you know! I care for you, Catriona. I admire your strength, and the passionate fire of your wayward spirit.'

Yet you have broken me! thought Catriona bitterly. *You are taking everything and leaving me with nothing of my own!*

'My inheritance!' she exclaimed suddenly, her plethora of confusion at once resolved. 'When I come of age and gain my inheritance, as my husband you will control my legacy!'

Catriona leaned across the white-clothed dining table towards Julian, her clear gaze challenging him to attempt a denial.

'Would you be so ardent to wed with me if I were to be permanently penniless, Julian?'

'Of course not,' he replied shortly. 'Due to my father's . . . mishandling . . . of certain events, marrying a wealthy wife is the only way in which I can ensure the future of both Pelham and the Espley Shipping Line.

'However, would *you* be marrying me — ' Julian grinned, neatly turning Catriona's question around upon her. ' — for any reason other than to save your precious Morgan Chappel's worthless skin?'

★ ★ ★

Some weeks later, despite the clear coldness of the morning, Huddy Unsworth's cheeks were scarlet and

154

shining. It was November 25th, and he was busily occupied shovelling the year's first snowfall from the cobbled yard of the coaching inn. Catriona stood waiting for the mail, absently watching the boy banking snow into grimy heaps, his brown collic-dog milling about his side as usual.

Huddy paused, leaning curiously on his spade, as a military detail cantered purposefully into the yard. The sergeant dismounted, striding into the inn to speak with the landlord, while the boy soldier accompanying him scurried to post printed notices upon the inn's wall and the doors of the smithy before continuing down the snowy road, tacking further notices at intervals onto the trunks of the gnarled, bare trees.

Huddy immediately tossed aside his spade and dashed to the wall, scrutinising the notice, with Toby barking and wagging excitedly beside him.

'It's Morgan, miss!' yelped Huddy, his eyes round and wide as he turned to look across at Catriona. 'I know it's him from the likeness, but what do it say, miss?'

She was already hurrying across the yard towards the notice, her knees weak with foreboding.

'It says Morgan has escaped from Castle Hill, Huddy,' she murmured with a sinking heart. 'A reward of two hundred guineas has been posted for his capture. Alive or — or — '

'A reward out for Morgan!' Huddy echoed in awe. 'Two hundred guineas! It's a fortune, miss! Somebody's bound to turn him in for that, aren't — miss?' He looked around in astonishment. Catriona was running from the icy yard out on to the road.

'Miss! Aren't you waiting for the mail?'

'Tomorrow, Huddy!' she called over her shoulder. 'I'll come again tomorrow!'

Catriona had not brought the wagon, lest its wheels become bogged in the deep snow drifts, so she hitched her skirts clear of her ankles and, leaving the road, started across country towards Pelham.

Julian was shaving when Catriona crashed into his room, her blood boiling.

'What devious, devilish thing have you done, Julian?' demanded Catriona furiously. 'Morgan's escaped from gaol. You told me he was to have gone free yesterday, but he's *escaped*! Morgan's a fugitive! There are wanted notices with his likeness drawn upon them posted everywhere — and a bounty of two hundred guineas for his capture, alive or dead!'

'Steady on, cousin!' remarked Julian smoothly, studying his reflection in the glass. 'You ought not burst into a man's bedroom when he's shaving. Any other time would be perfectly fine, but — '

'Don't you dare patronise me, Julian!' Catriona exploded. 'We had a pact!'

'I told you Morgan would go free.' Julian glanced around at her, all humour gone from his expression. 'He's free.'

'You're playing with words,' she retorted. 'Morgan's an escaped convict. A wanted man!'

'And whose fault is it that Morgan Chappel is a convict at all?' Julian goaded. 'Remember, sweet cousin, it was *your* testimony which first set the soldiers upon him! I did your bidding and got him out of Castle Hill by the only means possible — and much palm-greasing it took to do it!'

Catriona could not dispute the biting truth of Julian's taunts. 'He's sure to be captured, Julian,' she mumbled disconsolately. 'For two hundred guineas — '

' — most folk would betray their own mother,' Julian finished amiably. 'Yes, that's certainly true enough. However, by now, Morgan Chappel is many miles from Friars Quay.'

'Morgan's safe?' queried Catriona, her eyes suddenly alight with fearful hope. 'Are you absolutely certain of it?'

'Morgan went directly from Castle

Hill to the waterfront,' replied Julian smugly. 'Within one hour of his escape, he was sailing with the tide aboard a Dutch vessel bound for the Americas. Believe me, Catriona, he is already far from these shores!'

He laughed humourlessly. 'You really ought to thank me humbly and be exceedingly grateful!'

Catriona *was* grateful for Morgan's safekeeping. She was also incensed that Julian had played her every bit as adroitly as he'd control a pawn in one of his interminable games of chess.

Julian had manipulated her — and Morgan — so both were inextricably caught in the web he had contrived for them.

'You're very clever, Julian,' she commented, staring past him through the frost-feathered window pane. 'But don't assume I'm a complete fool. I see through your manipulative scheme! If Morgan had been properly released from gaol, he would be a truly free man, wouldn't he? Free to return to

Friars Quay, and to Pelham, in spite of the pact you and I have made. However, this way — the way you have arranged it . . . '

Julian spun around, his handsome features dark with rage. 'You're to be my *wife*! Never for a moment forget that, Catriona.' Reaching out, he caught her wrist within his strong fingers, pulling her roughly against him.

'I have your promise, and I fully intend on holding you to every word. And now, given the circumstances, you won't ever be tempted to seek out your lover, will you, sweet cousin?' Julian's mocking voice was cold and even. 'As for Morgan Chappel himself, he'll never come back to you, Catriona. Morgan understands only too well that all there is awaiting him in Friars Quay is the hangman's rope!'

★ ★ ★

Winter passed into spring, spring became summer, and folk in Friars

Quay forgot to watch every shadow and stranger lest it be Morgan Chappel. The Wanted notices faded and were tattered by wind and rain, blown away and lost from sight and mind.

Only Catriona remembered. Her first thoughts upon waking, her last before sleeping, were for Morgan.

Knowing he was lost to her forever blunted Catriona's senses, so she felt little — even at the prospect of her impending union with Julian.

She would be eighteen in but a few months, and Julian had informed her they were to be married before the year's end.

Catriona had long ago resigned herself to the situation. Determinedly suppressing every notion of self-pity or despair, she resolved to make the best of her marriage, and set to building as fruitful a life at Pelham as possible.

She was coming from the cottage beside the forge, having visited the smith's wife, who was poorly, when Huddy Unsworth raced across from the coaching inn, bursting with news.

'I've found out about Eliza, miss!' he blurted excitedly. 'On market day, it was! I heard some o' the wives talking. Eliza's gone to Hawksley Workhouse!

'The wives were saying how she'd got herself into trouble, miss.' Huddy frowned, scrubbing his chin with the back of his hand. 'Only I don't know what sort of trouble they meant.'

But Catriona guessed — Eliza was with child! *Morgan's* child . . .

She lost no time in sending a message to the officers of Hawksley, advising them she would visit the workhouse during the following afternoon.

Catriona told no one at Pelham of her intention to see Eliza; slipping cautiously from the stable, she drove the score or so miles inland to the market town of Hawksley.

None of the tales Catriona had heard about the parish workhouse had prepared her for the brutal reality of the institution. It was far worse than she could ever have imagined.

Despite all her jealousies and hostilities of the past, Catriona was glad she'd come to Hawksley. She could not allow Eliza to remain in such an iniquitous place, nor for Morgan's child to begin life here.

Catriona sat in the warden's room, waiting while Eliza was brought to her.

Once alone, there was silence.

Eliza glowered at Catriona from beneath lowered eyes.

'If you will permit me, Eliza,' ventured Catriona tentatively, 'I should like to help you, and your child.'

Eliza gave a bored shrug. 'Bairn's been taken.'

Catriona's heart froze. 'Taken?' she repeated fearfully.

'Oh, not dead, if that's what you're thinking, miss,' Eliza returned. 'Taken by a rich couple who likely can't have a lad of their own.'

Catriona's breath caught in her throat. Morgan had a son! But, oh, a

163

son he would never see; nor know, nor love!

'I reckon there's always takers for healthy baby boys,' Eliza was saying. She met Catriona's eyes defiantly. 'Fine boy, he was, miss.'

'I'm sure he was,' murmured Catriona wretchedly. 'If only I'd known! I could have helped you.'

'Whyever would you want to do that, miss?' Eliza mocked, her hard voice edged with contempt. 'You're to wed Mister Julian, aren't you?' she went on insolently. 'I suppose you fancy he loves you — well, he doesn't! He'll marry you for the same reason he'd have wed that old maid daughter of Judge Loxwood!'

'Eliza,' begged Catriona quietly, 'I don't want — '

'I don't give a fig what you don't want! You'll hear me out,' Eliza spat venomously. 'I'm not your skivvy anymore. I can say what I like, and I'll tell you summat I bet you've never even thought about!'

Her eyes narrowed spitefully, a sly grin curling her lips. 'The only reason Master asked you to Pelham was 'cause you're coming into money when you're twenty-one! Master knows what Mister Julian's like, and he reckoned if summat went wrong and Maud Loxwood didn't marry Julian, then he'd fix up a match between the pair of you. And that's the *only* reason Julian wants to wed with you, miss!'

Catriona wasn't at all taken aback by this revelation. Although it did surprise her slightly that her drunkard uncle had plotted so prudently and with such aforethought.

'Eliza, I'd like to offer you your old place at Pelham,' she said quietly. 'Will you come back?'

'You want to give me my job back?' Eliza queried warily. 'Even after what I just said to you, about Mister Julian and all? And what you know I've done?'

'I came to terms a long while ago with the fact that Morgan Chappel loved you,' answered Catriona softly.

'Yesterday, I discovered you'd borne his child.'

Eliza gave her a hard look, and chewed her lip thoughtfully.

'I only wish I had found out sooner,' Catriona concluded sadly. 'When you might have brought your son back with you.'

'Can't never go back to living in Friars Quay, miss,' Eliza said after a minute. 'I'd be shunned in the village. No lodgings would have me.'

'Then you need not set foot in the village,' Catriona replied decisively, rising from her seat. 'You may live-in at Pelham.'

10

Now, months later, Catriona was standing at her bedroom window, staring out across the shore fields and the cold, grey ocean.

Her wedding day had come. By nightfall, she would be Julian Espley's wedded wife. Mistress of Pelham.

And yet — Morgan Chappel was back!

She'd betrayed him, destroyed him. Why, oh why, was he risking his life to return?

Catriona spun around as her door swung open and Eliza hurried in, her pinched face paper-white and scared.

'I've just seen Mister Julian off to Liverpool,' she said agitatedly. 'But what about Morgan Chappel, miss? What are you going to do about *him*?'

'Morgan is a fugitive, Eliza.' began Catriona urgently, taking her cloak from its peg and hurriedly pulling it about her. 'He'll hang if he's captured. I have to find him!'

'Miss, don't say nothing to him about me!' Eliza implored, clasping Catriona's arm desperately. 'Or about the bairn!'

'Don't you want to see Morgan?' asked Catriona, perplexed by the maid's panic. 'Don't you still love him?'

'I don't give a fig for him, miss!' retorted Eliza shrilly. 'I'd be best suited if I never set eyes on him again for as long as I live!'

'Whatever you wish,' agreed Catriona with a sigh, her thoughts racing as she quit the room and clattered down the staircase with Eliza at her heels. 'You said you saw Morgan near the boat-house,' she said hurriedly, turning to Eliza before leaving the house. 'I'm going to find him and talk to him — but please tell no one about this, Eliza! Not Hannah or my uncle, nor Judge Loxwood and the military if they should call asking questions. And particularly not Julian — he mustn't know anything about your sighting of Morgan!'

With that, Catriona was gone; moving swiftly across the shore fields towards the beach; the soft surge of the receding tide, the cry of the gulls, and the spatter of rain borne by a keen north-westerly wind drumming in her ears. Cresting the dunes, Catriona froze in her tracks.

A dark, brooding figure was standing at the water's edge on the Marram Shore. He was gazing far out across the grey, shifting tide. With a stab of regret, Catriona realised it was almost the exact same place she had witnessed Morgan bearing the torch on the night *Isabella* was wrecked upon the Combs.

She moved downwards from the dunes. Morgan's back was turned to her. He was unaware of her approaching, and Catriona hesitated. Now so few yards stood between them, she was unsure what to do. What she could say to this man she had so treacherously betrayed?

As though sensing her presence, Morgan glanced around. With a cry wrung straight from her heart, Catriona ran to him. Morgan caught her fiercely up into his arms, his piercing blue eyes deeper than oceans and dark with the intensity of his longing for her.

Catriona raised her face to his, breathing his name over and over.

'This is the first time I've held you,' he whispered brokenly. 'But, Catriona, I've *loved* you . . . '

Morgan's words faded as he smoothed Catriona's tousled flaxen hair away from her face. 'You're crying!'

'I expected you to hate me,' she mumbled through glittering tears. 'I've betrayed you, and — and — '

Morgan's fingertips upon her lips tenderly silenced Catriona. 'You told what you saw, nothing more.'

'I was jealous — that's the reason I told Judge Loxwood where you were,' she confessed remorsefully. 'No matter what I'd seen that night on the beach, Morgan, I never believed you guilty of wrecking!'

'Then you were the only one!' he remarked bitterly. 'My presence there was damning. You once asked why I stayed at Pelham ... The answers I gave you were true, but there was another reason also. Long ago, I swore to someday clear my father's name and bring the Espleys to justice. To do that, I needed to be at Pelham.'

'I don't understand.' Catriona shook her head impatiently. 'How are my uncle and cousin connected with your father's being wrongly imprisoned?'

Morgan's lean face became grave. Reluctantly, he released her from his arms. 'So much has had to be unspoken between us, Catriona,' he began regretfully. 'And now we are finally together ... Well, now there are other things of greater importance which must be said immediately, for our time may be short.

'You have to know the whole truth

— although I pray I could spare you the pain much of it will undoubtedly bring.'

Catriona swallowed hard, slipping her arm through Morgan's and clasping his hand tightly.

'I've long suspected Julian of leading the Friars Quay smugglers,' Morgan began after a moment. 'That night, I'd followed him from Pelham to the beach. He disappeared into Spinney and I lost sight of him — '

'He'd seen you!' Catriona chipped in. 'For Julian came all the way back to Pelham to fetch me!'

'Julian's actions usually do have a shrewd logic behind them,' commented Morgan grimly. 'By the time I gave up searching Spinney for him and returned to the Marram Shore, the wreckers' light was burning and the *Isabella* was already on the Combs. Julian had succeeded in averting suspicion from himself and casting blame upon me at a single stroke!'

Morgan put a protective arm about Catriona's shoulders and they started walking along the desolate beach, with only the empty miles of sea and sand, the grassy crop of Gorse Cottage, and the high, rugged land of Beacon Point before them.

When he spoke again, Morgan's voice was indescribably gentle.

'Catriona, the *Isabella* is not the first ship the Espleys have wrecked.'

Catriona stared up at him with growing horror as she absorbed the full, terrible implication of Morgan's solemn words.

'Oh, no . . . no,' she whispered sorrowfully. 'Not *Rhiannon*?'

Morgan drew her close, until Catriona's cold cheek was resting against his chest.

'The *Rhiannon* was Samuel Espley's ship,' Morgan began carefully. 'She was to bring a shipment of gold ingots from New York to Liverpool. The gold was never put aboard. The crates contained only bars of worthless pig iron. Samuel Espley had devised an elaborate embezzlement, not only to steal the gold, but to swindle his insurers, too.

'He placed amongst *Rhiannon*'s crew a band of hand-picked villains. When the *Rhiannon* was far out to sea, these men were to mutiny. Take the ship off her course, and scuttle her in waters where her wreck would never be discovered. The mutineers planned to escape aboard a sister vessel, which would be lying by, and sail on to Jamaica.'

'My uncle would secretly have possession of the gold, while claiming its loss from his insurers?' Catriona reasoned bleakly. 'And claim for the loss of *Rhiannon* also, I suppose — a loss for which your father, as her captain, would be deemed responsible?'

'That was the Espleys' plan. Near foolproof it was, too. Except that my father uncovered the plot to mutiny and foiled it. Mutiny is a capital offence. When the perpetrators were cornered, they lost no time in naming Samuel Espley as author of the scheme,' related

Morgan. 'My pa wrote a full report into the *Rhiannon's* log, and he confided the details to *your* father, whose honour he respected.'

'Your father and mine knew each other?' queried Catriona in amazement.

'They'd sailed together often, and were firm friends,' Morgan replied with a reflective smile. 'It is strange to think of their knowing one another, isn't it? Being friends, all those years ago?'

Catriona nodded sadly, and Morgan held her even closer as they climbed the windswept dunes.

'*Rhiannon* proceeded along her true course,' he continued at length. 'When she was sighted safe and sound approaching Liverpool, Samuel and Julian were forced to take desperate measures. Once the ship docked, their part in the embezzlement and mutiny would be revealed. They had to ensure she never reached port,' he murmured, touching his lips tenderly to Catriona's throbbing temple. 'Between them, they lured

Rhiannon onto the rocks with a false light.

'I was here, just below Gorse Cottage, watching my father bringing his ship home — I *saw* Samuel and Julian Espley down on the beach with their wreckers' lantern.'

'They *murdered* my parents!' cried Catriona, her pain and anguish almost unbearable. 'Why are they still free? Why were they not arrested and punished?'

'*Proof*, Catriona! There isn't a shred of proof,' answered Morgan bitterly. 'Only the word of a disgraced ship's captain — and the eyewitness account of his eleven-year-old son!'

'The ship's log!' Catriona almost shouted. 'What of the report your father entered in the log? That's proof, isn't it?'

'Pa was depending upon the *Rhian-non*'s log being retrieved from the wreck and exonerating him,' said Morgan. 'Even the crates containing the bars of pig iron would have been proof enough to clear his name. But Samuel and Julian were leaving nothing to chance. Before official divers could arrive to make their search, the Espleys rowed out to the wreck in the dead of night, diving down upon her and setting explosive charges.

'They destroyed *Rhiannon* completely,' concluded Morgan, his anger undisguised. 'When the official divers went down a few days later, all they found of her was a flotsam of driftwood!'

'The Espleys got away with murder,' commented Catriona harshly. 'By blowing up the evidence against them!'

Morgan's jaw set stubbornly. 'They gutted the wreck, right enough, and Samuel Espley was injured in the process — but not before he had searched for and found *Rhiannon*'s log!'

'Are you certain about that?' she demanded quickly.

'No, not absolutely,' he admitted. 'However, I believe that ship's log is the reason your Aunt Amanda left Pelham and has never returned.'

'Amanda *knew* about the wrecking of *Rhiannon*?'

'Not at the time, nor for years afterwards. That much, I'm sure about. Amanda took me into her home after my mother died; she cared for me and made me one of the family. She was a good and kindly woman, Catriona,' he went on thoughtfully. 'I believe I know *exactly* when Amanda found out her husband and son were responsible for the wrecking.

'It was one particular night. Amanda and Samuel were attending a ball given by the Loxwoods at Larks Grange. I was still only a lad, and I used to like seeing all the finery and the fancy carriages and horses and suchlike — Pelham was a splendid place in those days. Anyhow, I stayed awake to wait for them coming home from the ball.

'I was watching from the landing. Amanda looked as beautiful as always in her French gown and jewels, but

Samuel was rather drunk and had to be helped to bed by his valet.

'Amanda was left to return her jewels to the drawing-room safe, a task she never did herself, since Samuel always insisted upon opening and closing the safe personally.'

Morgan's clear blue eyes were burning with conviction.

'I'm convinced Amanda found *Rhiannon*'s log in that safe, Catriona! Or, if not the log, some other evidence that incriminated the Espleys in the vessel's wrecking. Because the very next morning, she left Pelham and took your cousin Lucy with her!'

'If you're right, then Amanda can testify — '

'If Amanda didn't go to the authorities then, she won't now,' replied Morgan firmly. 'She might have been unable to continue living under the same roof as Samuel and Julian, but she couldn't send her husband and son to the gallows, either!'

'Do you suppose the ship's log still

exists?' Catriona ventured eagerly, the germ of an idea in her mind. 'Do you?'

Morgan shrugged. 'After Amanda left, I never was able to get into the drawing-room, much less tackle trying to open the safe!'

'I could try!' she cried fervently. 'I could slip in and — '

'Absolutely not!' Morgan interrupted. 'I wouldn't have told you any of this, had I thought you'd respond in a foolhardy way! Make no mistake, Catriona — if you cross the Espleys, your life won't be worth a candle!'

'Finding the ship's log is the only chance of ending this!' she retorted stubbornly.

'No! Don't even attempt searching, Catriona!' forbade Morgan crisply. 'There is another possibility for reaching the truth.

'After escaping from Castle Hill, I was put aboard a Dutch brig bound for the Americas. I jumped ship at Land's End, and I've been scouring the ports for the few sailors who survived

Rhiannon's wrecking.'

'Of course — there were other survivors besides your father and myself!' exclaimed Catriona, adding doubtfully, 'Weren't they questioned at the time, though?'

'They were. And either they didn't know anything, or were too intimidated by Samuel Espley's power and reputation to speak against him,' replied Morgan grimly. 'So far, I've tracked down only one of *Rhiannon*'s sailors — a sick old man who is still too afraid to bear witness against the Espleys. The wrecking happened many years ago, but fear lasts a long time.

'There are other survivors, though,' he finished decisively. 'I'll find them eventually.'

Catriona reached up; sadly, tentatively, touching Morgan's mouth with her lips.

'You're in peril every moment you're here in Friars Quay,' she murmured. 'Why have you come back?'

'I *had* to! When I learned of your

betrothal, I had to come! Don't you understand, Catriona?' Morgan went on vehemently. 'I can't bear even the notion of your becoming Julian Espley's wife!'

'Go away, Morgan! Please, please, go away,' she begged, desperate in her fears for his life and tearing herself from the sweet temptation of his nearness. 'Don't you see, it's too late — nothing can stop this marriage now!'

* * *

Downcast and deeply troubled by her anxieties for Morgan, Catriona's heart sank in dismay when she stole through the November dusk back into Pelham's yard and saw Redbird cropping the tough grass outside the stables.

Julian was already home from Liverpool.

The kitchen door opened, spilling light across the cobbles. Eliza darted out to meet her.

'Did you see Morgan, miss?' she

queried agitatedly. 'Where is he?'

'I'm not sure,' Catriona replied despondently. 'Gone, I pray.'

Catriona and Eliza went together up into the house. Even from the kitchen, Catriona could hear the irate raised voices of Julian and his father arguing behind the closed doors of the drawing-room.

'Did Julian notice I wasn't here?' asked Catriona.

'Huh! Too busy going at it hammer and tongs with the Master!' Eliza retorted. 'Just hark at the pair of 'em!'

For once, Catriona actually welcomed the animosity between the Espleys.

'The Master's already had a drop or twenty,' Eliza went on scornfully. 'By the wedding, he'll be proper three sheets to the wind! Mind, there's nowt queer 'bout that, is there, miss?'

Catriona gave a resigned sigh, sinking wearily into the chimney corner. Hunching her knees up close against her chest, she closed her eyes, burying her face into her folded arms exactly as she had when she was a small, dejected child.

But she was no longer a child. Catriona was a young woman, and the responses the touch of Morgan Chappel's hands and lips had awakened were still aching unfulfilled deep within her.

'You love him, don't you, miss?' Eliza blurted suddenly. 'Morgan, I mean!'

'Yes.' Catriona half-smiled, her answer barely a whisper. 'I believe I always have, and always will.'

'Thought as much.' Eliza chewed her lip, deliberating. 'You've been good to me, miss, fetching me from the workhouse and all. I owe you summat for that.'

'You don't owe me, Eliza.' Catriona shook her head soberly. 'Not a thing.'

'Begging your pardon, miss, but I reckon I do. And that I ought to tell you summat,' began Eliza, glancing around to make certain Hannah was still occupied in the pantry and well out of earshot. 'It's about Morgan Chappel and me . . . '

11

'That night, miss — the night *Isabella* got wrecked — Mister Julian turned up at my lodgings in the village,' Eliza began hesitantly. 'He had a scheme, you see, to get rid of Morgan once and for all.'

The maid avoided Catriona's anxious eyes. 'Julian said he'd make me housekeeper if I did exactly like he told me.'

Catriona caught her breath. 'What did he want you to do, Eliza?'

'I had to come back to Pelham and make sure nobody saw me,' she continued in a low voice. 'After Morgan got back from the beach and went up to bed in the hayloft, I was to hide in the stables and wait. When Julian gave the signal, I had to hang on a minute or two, then sneak out of the stables and make it look like I'd just . . . like

. . . well, you *know*, miss.

'But it wasn't that way at all!' Eliza cried, her voice rising. 'Morgan Chappel didn't even know I was in the stables that night! There wasn't ever anything happened between me and Morgan,' she concluded fervently. 'Not that night, nor never!'

Catriona stared at Eliza blankly, not quite knowing what to make of the maid's emotional outburst. 'But what of your child?' she asked after a pause. 'Your son?'

'He wasn't Morgan Chappel's, miss.' Eliza looked away uncomfortably, her words dropping so low Catriona could barely hear them. 'My bairn was Mister Julian's.'

Catriona's full attention snapped back upon the maid. 'Does Julian know?'

'I should say he does!' retorted Eliza scathingly. 'Why do you reckon he had the Master dismiss me from Pelham?'

'The deceitful, selfish, heartless . . . ' Catriona bit her lip. 'How *could* he

187

condemn you and his own flesh and blood to that — that — vile, godforsaken institution?'

'Out of sight, out of mind, I reckon, miss.' Eliza shrugged matter-of-factly. 'It was — Tea's still hot, miss!' She hastily changed the subject as the kitchen door banged open. 'Sure you won't have a cup?'

'Tea? There's no time for tea parties, girl!' Julian remarked, striding into the kitchen and bending to kiss Catriona's forehead. 'Shouldn't you be making ready, sweet cousin? We leave within the hour!'

'I shall be ready,' replied Catriona stiffly, rising from the chimney corner. 'Eliza will assist me.'

'I will, miss.' Eliza bobbed a curtsey to Julian and scurried around him into the hall.

Catriona made to follow, but as she moved past Julian, he outstretched his hand across her hips, arresting her in mid-stride.

'I'm eagerly anticipating our union,

Catriona,' he murmured against her ear. 'Unfortunately, the old man insists upon accompanying us to church. However, since he's embarking upon a gambling and supping jag directly after, we shall be free to relish the first hours of our marriage alone.'

'Excuse me, Julian,' Catriona said crisply, turning away from him. 'I have to change.'

★　★　★

Once within her mistress's room, Eliza hurriedly shut the door fast and spun round to Catriona, her thin face animated and aghast.

'You're never still going to wed him, miss?' she exclaimed. 'You can't be!'

'Oh, but I am,' replied Catriona evenly. 'I must.'

The prospect of marrying Julian was now more appalling, more repugnant to her than ever before. Yet surely becoming irrevocably wedded to Julian Espley was the only means Catriona possessed of deterring Morgan Chappel from ever again returning to Friars Quay?

Catriona turned calmly to the maid. 'Eliza, please fetch my dress.'

The November night was icy, and Catriona's empty heart colder still as she drove with Julian to her wedding.

The carriage wheels crunched through frost lying thick upon the rough ground, and the rising moon was near to fullness, blurred with a gauzy halo. Its chill brilliance spilled stark upon white ribbons of water frozen into stillness along the roadside ditches.

Throughout the drive, Catriona scanned the shadow-filled landscape for any glimpse of Morgan Chappel. Since setting off from Pelham, she'd had an uncanny, fearful sense Morgan was nearby, and her only emotion at reaching the small Norman church was intense relief that her ominous presentiment was wrong. Morgan had not appeared.

Going up the church steps, Catriona glanced back over her shoulder into the bleak winter's night. Perhaps, after all, Morgan was indeed long gone from Friars Quay . . .

The church was lit only by a solitary branch of candles. Shadows clung to the corners and alcoves; the altar was bare of flowers, the rows of dark pews empty.

Samuel slumped into a pew close to the aisle, while Julian took Catriona's hand and led her to the altar.

'Enough of your cantish babble, Burwick!' Julian muttered, irritably interrupting the minister as he commenced reading from the book of prayers. 'Get on with it, can't you — '

'There'll be no marriage this night — nor any other!'

The soft voice had eerie resonance as it echoed up to the heights of the ancient stone church.

Morgan!

Catriona stood absolutely still at the altar, not daring to even glance around.

However, in that fleeting instant, regardless of her anxiety for Morgan's safety, Catriona's heart sang!

Morgan was *here*. Somehow, in some way, they *would* be together. Catriona would be his — and his alone!

'Morgan Chappel!' Julian's face twisted into an ugly sneer. 'So, even a bounty of two hundred guineas upon your life could not keep you away from your little playmate!'

'You're not going to marry Catriona,' announced Morgan calmly, stepping from the shadows of the rear alcove. 'You're a murderer and a wrecker, Julian. Exactly like your father.'

Samuel Espley suddenly lurched to his feet, rounding upon his son.

'Damn you, Julian!' he swayed drunkenly, falling back into the pew. 'Damn you to eternal hell! Didn't I tell you? But you were so clever!' He spat derisively. 'You had to twist the knife, get your revenge — '

Neither Morgan nor Julian were paying any attention to Samuel Espley.

Their concentration was focused on one another — and upon Catriona, who stood between them in her wedding gown.

Morgan strode along behind the rear pews towards the aisle, and Catriona felt Julian's hold about her waist tighten.

'I shall presently delight in delivering you to Judge Loxwood and claiming the two hundred guineas' purse for your corpse, Morgan,' he taunted.

Catriona sensed his swift, almost imperceptible movement. Glimpsed the dull gleam of candlelight upon gun-metal as Julian withdrew a sidearm, levelling the snub pistol at Morgan Chappel's heart.

'Meanwhile,' he continued smoothly. 'The marriage proceeds!'

Reverend Burwick nervously licked a dry tongue over his lips.

'No,' the clergyman declared at last, steadfastly closing the prayer book. 'I'm not a brave man, Mister Espley, but I'll not condone your profanity of the

Lord's holy place, nor hear your vows of matrimony!'

Julian threw Burwick a scornful glower as the minister hastened to quit the church, while the pistol's aim remained steadily trained upon Morgan Chappel.

'You shall pay for this interference with your life,' commented Julian, looking his adversary square in the face. 'I'm calling you!'

Catriona saw an unexpected smile play wryly upon Morgan's lips.

'So, you fear what I may now have to tell Judge Loxwood?' queried the Welshman smoothly. 'And seek to silence me by exacting the Espleys' particular brand of retribution!'

'Choose your weapons,' Julian challenged. 'If you have steel and stomach enough for the encounter, that is!'

'Pistols.' Morgan's rejoinder was terse.

'So be it.' Julian pushed Catriona ahead of him as they started back down the aisle.

Morgan stepped away, leaving their path clear. However, as they drew level, Catriona twisted free from Julian's hold upon her waist and coldly rounded on him.

'I'm *never* going back to Pelham with you!'

'You'll do as I tell you,' Julian remarked indifferently. 'You're still a minor, and my father is your guardian. Which effectively means — ' He carelessly indicated Samuel Espley's inebriated staggering from the church. ' — that *I* am your guardian, Catriona. And also your only living relative!'

Julian's gaze snapped to Morgan, and Catriona could not comprehend the intelligence which transferred between the two men.

'Do not entertain the notion of spiriting my wayward cousin from Pelham by stealth of this night, Morgan,' continued Julian urbanely. 'I shall shoot you down as a trespasser, and as for Catriona — I admit to desiring the girl for my wife, but if anything unfortunate *were* to befall her . . . ' His full lips curled into a cruel smile. ' . . . Catriona would still be worth every shilling as much to me!'

'Neither your greed nor your threats intimidate me!' professed Catriona — untruthfully, for she could scarce prevent herself trembling. 'I shall not go with you, Julian!'

'Go, Catriona!' ordered Morgan evenly. 'Return to Pelham — and make no attempt to leave.'

'Your rustic playmate guides you wisely, cousin,' Julian remarked, ushering her from the church. Pausing on the weathered steps and donning his hat, he tugged its brim in mock salute to Morgan Chappel.

'I look forward to our meeting upon Beacon Point . . . '

* * *

Neither Catriona nor Julian uttered a single word during the drive out to Pelham. However, when they were

196

inside the house and Catriona was about to retire to her room, she allowed herself the indulgence of begging for an explanation of that which had troubled her since leaving the village church.

'Julian, why are you and Morgan to meet at Beacon Point?'

'Oh, sweet innocent cousin! You genuinely don't understand, do you?' He laughed mirthlessly, taking her cold hand and pressing it to his lips. 'At sunrise, Chappel and I will end our differences once and for ever — by the noble art of *duelling*!'

Catriona sedately climbed the stairs, but once away from Julian's keen gaze, she fled trembling along the landing into her bedroom; firmly turning the key in the lock lest Julian, in the brutality of his present mood, should seek entry.

For all her resolute determination of past months, Catriona now felt as helpless and vulnerable — as hopelessly and inexorably trapped — as she had during her earliest days with the Espleys.

Steeling her nerve, Catriona summoned every ounce of inner strength to suppress the panic-stricken, dreadful emotions surging within her. She fastened her thoughts upon the imminent duel — and the need for her to somehow prevent its occurring.

Whatever could she *do*?

Compelling herself to act methodically, Catriona lit her lamp; changed from the wedding dress into her sturdy everyday clothing; and then sat beside the window, her fingers anxiously knotted into her lap as she racked her mind for a solution.

Heedless of Morgan's dire warning, Catriona finally realised exactly what she must do.

Moving noiselessly from the window to her bed, Catriona lay down. Far too tense to sleep, she stared up at the ceiling, listening for Julian to retire.

It was long past midnight before she heard his footsteps upon the landing.

He paused outside her room, and Catriona blessed the lock that would hold the door fast if needed. However, Julian did not try to enter, his footfalls presently continuing on along the landing.

Catriona crept to the door. There was not a moment to be lost. Inching open the door, she cautiously peered out on to the landing. Julian had passed beyond his own master bedroom, and was letting himself into Eliza's box-room, hungry for familiar comforts.

Catriona waited only a second longer before stealing downstairs.

Once in Samuel Espley's drawing-room, she lit her lamp and made for the safe.

She immediately guessed it would store nothing of value, for the locking device was broken. The safe's door swung freely open, and Catriona quickly rifled through the dog-eared bundles of worthless papers inside.

She stood, hands pressed to her hips in exasperation.

Which other secure hidey-hole was there? Where would Samuel Espley secrete something as dangerously valuable as the *Rhiannon*'s log?

Catriona slipped off her shoes, speeding up the stairs again.

If the log still existed, Julian would no longer risk entrusting such incriminating evidence to his father's safekeeping!

And if the ship's log *did* still exist, then surely Julian Espley himself would have possession of it?

Inside the master bedroom, Catriona closed the door soundlessly, and with hammering heart surveyed the large room.

The oak secretary in the fireplace alcove!

Seconds later, the salt-stained, water-blurred log of the brigantine *Rhiannon* was hers!

The drawer also contained sundry other documents. Dates; names; places; columns of figures. Julian obviously kept scrupulous records of his contrabanding activities — together with a deal of incriminating material that might be used for blackmailing both adversaries and associates, should the need ever arise.

There was, in addition, the solid gold seal of the *Isabella* — and only one way in which Julian Espley could have obtained it.

Galvanised by the striking of the distant church clock, and reminded of the scant remaining hours before dawn, Catriona quit the master bedroom. Darting into her own room, she retrieved her amethyst brooch, for — if her plans ran well — she was well aware that after this ghastly night was over, she might never again be beneath Pelham's gabled roofs.

Out from the house; across the cobbled yard and into the stables. Catriona patted the mild-mannered grey, speaking softly to the mare as she passed along the row of stalls to Redbird.

The spirited thoroughbred shifted restlessly as Catriona's cold, unsure fingers fumbled with the numerous buckles and straps of bridle and saddle. Once out in the crisp, cold night air, however, Redbird whickered and tossed her head, responding instinctively to Catriona's feather-light touch upon the reins and galloping effortlessly for the Marram Shore.

Morgan was nowhere in sight, and with night already ebbing towards daybreak, Catriona could not tarry longer in search of him.

Heading up amongst the dunes and into Spinney, Catriona rode like the wind for Larks Grange to rouse Judge Loxwood.

The first threads of dawn were lighting the eastern sky as Catriona and Beverell Loxwood made haste towards the beach. Catriona marveled that the elderly gentleman had paid any heed to the dishevelled young woman pounding at his door in the wee small hours!

However, even if Judge Loxwood hadn't comprehended much of Catriona's garbled explanations, the ship's log and other documents which she had placed into his custody made sense enough for the judge to immediately direct a messenger to the garrison, requesting that the military converge with all possible speed upon Beacon Point.

Emerging from the scrub pines and climbing the inland-facing, rugged gradient of the Point, Catriona was distraught to sight five men already assembled out on the windswept crest of high land.

'They've begun!' Judge Loxwood cautioned her in a low voice. 'Be silent, Miss Dunbar. They must have no distraction.'

Catriona stifled her cry of anguish. After everything that had happened, after all she'd tried to do, she was still too late to stop the duel taking place!

Morgan and Julian Espley were standing back-to-back, pistols raised against their chests. Archibald Liddle's voice carried distinctly on the keen November wind as the physician counted out the ten paces before the duellists would turn and fire their weapons.

The crack of pistol shot tore apart the dawn silence.

Catriona cried out. Saw Morgan half-crouching, spinning around. Julian was standing squarely, already facing Morgan, a thread of acrid smoke curling from the muzzle of his raised and discharged pistol.

All Catriona saw and understood was that Morgan was alive and safe!

'It's far from over, Miss Dunbar.' Judge Loxwood's authoritative tone bludgeoned Catriona's euphoria. 'Your cousin fired his weapon prematurely. *Dishonourably*,' added the judge in disgust. 'Julian Espley is a cheat and a coward.'

'I care nothing for what he is, Judge Loxwood!' cried Catriona in frustrated exasperation. 'May I go and tell Morgan the news? That he is exonerated from all charges, and his father's name has at last been cleared?'

'In a moment, Miss Dunbar. In a moment,' replied the elderly gentleman mildly. 'The duel must run its course. Morgan will aim and fire at his leisure.'

'Morgan won't do that!' protested Catriona incredulously. 'He'd never shoot — '

'He must,' Judge Loxwood cut in evenly. 'Espley is disgraced, his name and family shamed. Unless Espley faces Morgan Chappel's fire, he shall not redeem a shred of honour!'

'The Espleys are beyond shame, Judge Loxwood,' murmured Catriona, her attention fixed upon the grim scene being played to its finale upon Beacon Point. 'Their decency and honour is long past any redemption.'

'Hold your fire, Morgan!' Julian's call to his adversary was low and tense. 'What gain is there in your killing me? Every man has his price — and I know yours!

'The girl!' He grinned confidently. 'Spare my life, and Catriona's yours.'

Morgan remained silent.

205

'What of your father, Morgan?' persisted Julian. His throat was tight, his face wet with cold sweat. 'He's been in gaol a long while. He's getting old, Morgan! May not have much time left. You could get him out, clear his name — with help from me!'

Morgan raised the pistol a fraction, keeping its barrel steadily levelled at Julian Espley.

'I have *Rhiannon*'s log, Morgan!' Julian continued, staring transfixed across the ten paces directly into the pistol's barrel. 'Iron-clad proof of my own father's guilt.'

Morgan still said nothing; but, drawing back the hammer of his pistol, he slowly took aim — and discharged the shot harmlessly into the sandy ground.

'My quest was not for vengeance, Julian,' he said at length, throwing the smoking pistol aside and striding from the Point. 'Only for justice!'

Catriona broke away from Judge Loxwood, flying to Morgan. Unable even to speak, she buried her face into his chest, holding Morgan to her as though she would never let him go.

She was scarcely aware of the red-coated soldiers galloping over the rise, fanning out and swiftly closing in to arrest Julian Espley as he lunged for Redbird's reins and made one final frantic bid for escape.

'Miss Dunbar, Mister Chappel!' Judge Loxwood cleared his throat, approaching the embracing couple briskly. 'The Captain of the Command advises me that within the last hour, the body of Samuel Espley has been discovered in Briarley Brook. It is uncertain,' the judge concluded solemnly, 'whether Espley suffered an accident and drowned, or deliberately took his own life.'

Later that morning, when pale winter sunlight gleamed upon the lapping slate-grey waves of the incoming tide, Catriona and Morgan wandered together upon the wild, desolate Marram Shore.

Pausing at the old boathouse, Morgan drew Catriona nearer. She responded instinctively: moving against him, wanting to hear his every breath, longing to feel the beat of his heart so close to her own.

'Will you marry me, Catriona?' he murmured, stroking the softness of her hair. 'Will you?'

Catriona met Morgan's clear blue eyes, her fingertips tenderly exploring every contour of his face and mouth.

When she touched her lips to his, the warmth of Catriona's kiss offered Morgan Chappel every answer he desired . . .

We do hope that you have enjoyed reading this large print book.

Did you know that all of our titles are available for purchase?

We publish a wide range of high quality large print books including:
Romances, Mysteries, Classics
General Fiction
Non Fiction and Westerns

Special interest titles available in large print are:
The Little Oxford Dictionary
Music Book, Song Book
Hymn Book, Service Book

Also available from us courtesy of Oxford University Press:
Young Readers' Dictionary
(large print edition)
Young Readers' Thesaurus
(large print edition)

For further information or a free brochure, please contact us at:
Ulverscroft Large Print Books Ltd.,
The Green, Bradgate Road, Anstey,
Leicester, LE7 7FU, England.
Tel: (00 44) **0116 236 4325**
Fax: (00 44) **0116 234 0205**